Kasey & Ivy

Alison Hughes

Kasey & Ivy

ORCA BOOK PUBLISHERS

Library and Archives Canada Cataloguing in Publication

Hughes, Alison, 1966–, author
Kasey & Ivy / Alison Hughes.

Issued in print and electronic formats.
ISBN 978-1-4598-1574-2 (softcover).—ISBN 978-1-4598-1575-9 (pdf)—
ISBN 978-1-4598-1576-6 (epub)

I. Title. II. Title: Kasey and Ivy.
PS8615.U3165K37 2018   jc813'.6   C2017-904560-1
C2017-904561-x

First published in the United States, 2018
Library of Congress Control Number: 2017949722

Summary: In this middle-grade novel, twelve-year-old Kasey spends a month in the geriatric ward of her local hospital and strikes up some unusual friendships.

Orca Book Publishers is dedicated to preserving the environment and has printed this book on Forest Stewardship Council® certified paper.

Orca Book Publishers gratefully acknowledges the support for its publishing programs provided by the following agencies: the Government of Canada through the Canada Book Fund and the Canada Council for the Arts, and the Province of British Columbia through the BC Arts Council and the Book Publishing Tax Credit.

Edited by Sarah N. Harvey
Cover artwork by Julie McLaughlin

ORCA BOOK PUBLISHERS
www.orcabook.com

Printed and bound in Canada.

21 20 19 18 • 4 3 2 1

For Jen

One

Dear Nina,

I know this must be weird, getting a handwritten letter from me when we live next door to each other and see each other practically all the time. I can picture you looking confused. But stop what you're doing, stop even *chewing* (if you're eating), and read this.

This has been the worst day of my life. Truly. In some ways, it's been even more dramatic than when we had that tornado warning at school. Remember? It got all dark and the sky was *greenish* and it looked as if we were in the middle of a legit catastrophe, but all that really happened was that the wind howled through the cracks in the portable, Brianna cried, Mrs. D. got all nervous and blotchy and our parents had to pick us up early. Your dad came to get you before things really got exciting. We had a thrilling dash through the pouring rain to our van. Did you know that I even carried Molly? I did. She's heavier than she looks. And she was wet weight. I know she could have run, but she was upset, and Mom had the baby and Kyle, so I piggybacked her. Lizzy carried the backpacks and the diaper bag, plodding after us to the van. We were all *soaked*. To the skin! We listened to the *thuk-thuk* of shoes banging around the dryer the rest of the week.

Wow, give me a pen and paper, and I'll just write and write.

You'll never guess where I'm going right now, Nina.

To the hospital!

Truth. I, Kasey Morgan, am going to be a genuine, hospital-bracelet-wearing patient. Here's how it happened. You know that thing on my leg? The red bump I showed you near my ankle?

2

Below the soccer bruise I got when that cheap-shotter Samantha Skinner slide-tackled me illegally when I was crossing the ball in that game we lost 2–1 against Carson Heights? Well, after weeks and weeks of it getting bigger and redder, we finally went to the doctor. And when I say "we," I mean all of us, other than Dad, who was at work. You've known the Morgan family all your life, Nina. You know we do everything in a lurching, messy, screaming group. Even a doctor's appointment. It's so embarrassing.

"Kasey, you sit up there," my mom said, sitting down in the only chair. She had the baby on her shoulder and Kyle squirming on her lap. She pointed over at the long stretcher-thingy with that thin sheet of paper over top that can't possibly keep you safe from other people's germy diseases. First of all, it's not wide enough. Don't the paper people ever measure? There's a good three inches of stretcher on either side of the paper that stays completely uncovered and must be just *crawling* with germs. Second of all, you can see through the paper, it's that thin. You think see-through paper

3

is going to stop germs and bacteria from crawling up your legs? No way. I've seen the nature shows. Those things are survivors.

Lizzy and Molly hopped up there on the diseasy paper with me, because there was no other place for them to sit or even stand really. Examination rooms were not built for six people plus a doctor. And they weren't built for little kids waiting for ages for a doctor to arrive. Kyle ripped almost all the pages out of a magazine and tossed Cheerios around like confetti. That boy gives new meaning to the term "terrible two." Mom was feeding the baby under a blanket when someone double-knocked, then banged open the door and barged right in.

"Oho, so the whole family's here!" the doctor said in this loud, jolly voice, smiling and showing us all her huge, crooked teeth. Obviously, we were all here. Too many of us.

"How many of you *are* there?" she went on, smiling at us. This was a doctor I'd never seen before. She did not inspire confidence, Nina. She started banging around in a cupboard, knocking over a cup of tongue depressors, and finally brought out some zoo-animal stickers that she handed around.

"No, thank you," I said coldly when she came around to me. Seriously? I'm *twelve years old.*

"Ah, you must be"—she looked down at the sheet she'd crumpled in her hand—"Katherine-Charlotte."

"Technically," I said. *You* know that's my name, Nina, and how I shortened it to K.C. for a while and then it just morphed into Kasey. And how I finally, actually, like my name, because now I don't sound like some kid in a pioneer bonnet. ("Pa's bringin' in the cattle, Katherine-Charlotte, y'hear?") But very, very few other people know my real name. Don't tell anybody else. Only doctors and substitute teachers call me Katherine-Charlotte.

"She goes by Kasey," Mom said quickly, seeing the look on my face. She patted the baby on the back and gave a nervous little laugh. Even after having five babies (maybe *because* of having five babies), Mom is still super nervous of anything medical. Well, you've seen our home remedies, Nina. We've talked about them. You have normal parents who go to clinics and pharmacies, so it's hard for you to understand why somebody would use apple cider vinegar on a wart (for example). We've been using something called witch hazel on the steadily growing red bump on my ankle. Seriously. Let me tell you, whatever witchcraft this Hazel uses, it doesn't work.

Anyway, in between the baby screaming and Mom shushing and burping him, and Kyle bugging Molly, and Lizzy trying to referee those two, the doctor poked at my leg. At first she was pretty casual, gripping it with her big, dry hand. But then she crouched down and looked at it very closely and carefully. I preferred it when she was casual. She got so serious that it made me nervous. She started firing questions at me. What day did the bruise happen? How soon after the bruise did the red lump appear? Was it painful? Sensitive to the touch? I could tell my mom was straining to hear what we were saying over the baby's screaming.

The doctor finally straightened up and sat back heavily in her wheely-chair.

"Kasey," the doctor said, "you're the big girl in the family, I see. Grade—what? Six? I should say just *finishing* sixth grade."

I nodded. This was not going to be good. Whenever adults remind you that you're a big girl, it means they don't want a screamer. It means serious trouble.

Nina, I swear my heart was thumping so hard I could hardly hear anything else. My face was hot, all I could hear was the *whoosh-whoosh* of my heartbeat, and my hands were clammy. I missed the first part of what she said.

"—so you'll understand that we have to do some tests on this lump of yours. In the hospital."

"The *hos*pital!" Mom blurted.

"Yes. She needs a bone scan as soon as possible. Today, in fact, if I can get her in on an emergency basis. The scanner is at the Royal Vic, not at the local hospital," said the doctor.

"A *bone* scan!"

Mom didn't mean to be annoying. She really didn't.

"They're going to *scan* Kasey's *bones*?" I heard Molly's too-loud, horrified voice say beside me. "But her bones are *inside her body!*" She's only four, right? So this all must have seemed super scary to her. Not only to her, actually.

"Shhh," Lizzy whispered back. "It's probably an X-ray thing. To see inside her. Shhh. It'll be okay."

The doctor wrote on a form. My first impression of her was changing. At first this doctor seemed clumsy, incompetent and in need of a good dentist. Between her and the witch hazel, I might have chosen the witch. But now, with her face set and serious, she was all business. And way scarier.

She handed the sheet over to my mother and left to find somebody to scan my bones. A bone scanner. Doesn't *that* sound like a creepy profession, Nina?

I looked at Mom, and Mom looked at me, and both of us looked scared and worried. But we gave each other tight, brave smiles to try to convince each other that we weren't.

"It's going to be fine. Just fine," Mom said, slipping a soother into the baby's mouth.

"But her bones! Kasey's *bones!*" Molly wailed, throwing out her little arms for emphasis.

"My bones are *fine.*" I said it firmly and loudly, trying to convince everyone. Trying to convince myself.

We poured out of the little room and waited in the waiting room. Mom called Dad while Kyle hopped on one foot, repeating the word *bones* eight million times, making it into a bouncing song. "Bones, bones, bones, bones, bones…"

"Dad's coming from work in a few minutes to drive you to the hospital," Mom said. We sat and stared at the door. When Dad came in, Mom ran over to him, talking quick and low. Then she came over to me, and while the baby grabbed a tight handful of my hair, she kissed the top of my head and smooshed me into her hip in a fierce, awkward hug.

"Everything's going to be just fine, Pumpkin. Just *fine.*" Her voice sounded funny.

She untangled the baby, turned and grabbed Kyle mid-hop and said, "Let's go, girls" in that same fake-cheerful voice. Lizzy grabbed Molly's hand, turned at the door and waved at me. Good old Lizzy. She's only eight, but I'd give Lizzy the Most Responsible Morgan Award. Absolutely 100 percent. I'll bet you she could even drive the van if she really had to.

"Okay, Pumpkin," Dad said, coming back from the desk with a folder of papers. "Got all the paperwork. Let's go find out what the heck that lump is." He smiled, but I could tell he was worried.

We are both quiet as we drive to the Royal Vic, a monster hospital in the scary, run-down part of the city. I keep wondering how I got a scanner appointment so quickly. Don't people wait for months for things like that? Is this some discount, cheapo scanner? Or am I really an emergency case?

Anyway, my bones, bones, bones are speeding closer to the hospital with the scanner.

What does a scanner do, exactly?

I wonder if it hurts.

Your nervous friend with a possibly diseased leg bone,
Kasey

TWO

Dear Nina,

I'm back.

I was told to sit in this very disgusting hospital waiting room. The Emergency room. As the name indicates, it is not a fun party room. It's more of a Crisis room, a Catastrophe room. It's where all the people who can't wait to see a regular doctor go. Very sick people or those who are actively gushing blood, for example. Which I'm not. There was a crumpled, used-looking Kleenex on one of the seats. There was also some sort of evil smear on the magazine beside me. I didn't want to look at it, but I couldn't seem to stop myself.

Dad had to go move the car. There were no spots anywhere, so Dad just lurched the car up to the door. According to a very large security guard, he had "three minutes" to get me in here and come back to move it.

"She'll be just fine," said a big clerk with long nails that must be hard to type with. "I'll keep an eye on her. She'll be heading in for her scan shortly."

"Go, Dad," I hissed. "That guy's going to tow the car!"

"Back in a flash." He gave my hand a painful squeeze and sprinted back to the doors.

I looked around the waiting room. A really old woman sat staring straight ahead of her, looking angry. She had tightly curled hair and held her purse with both hands on her lap like somebody was going to snatch it. A woman with a terrible cough flipped through a magazine and spewed disease into the room with each cough. I turned my head and tried not to breathe her germy air. I breathed away from her, in little panting breaths. There was a terribly thin man in a wheelchair who had his eyes closed. Another guy was completely bent over, clutching his stomach.

I sat and listened to the *tick-tick-tick* of the clerk typing, snuck glances at the smeary magazine beside me and stared down at my sandals. I wished I had shoes that shut out diseases rather than ones that left my toes right out there in the germy open. I looked around for some hand sanitizer. I couldn't very well scrub my feet, but I could clean my hands. Nothing. Can you believe that? No hand sanitizer in a *hospital*, Nina! I was not feeling cheerful about any part of this experience.

A porter with a wheelchair grabbed a binder at the desk, then shuffled out to the waiting area.

"Katherine-Charlotte?" he croaked.

The porter was so old, I didn't know who would be pushing who for a minute there. Not just old— ancient. Way, *way* older than my grandparents.

"In you get," he wheezed, bending super slowly to push down the footrests.

"Actually, I can walk fine," I said, thinking there must have been some mistake.

The porter gave me a dark look and turned to confer with Tappy Nails at the desk. I heard him mutter "attitude." The clerk came around the desk.

"Now, Katherine-Charlotte," she said in a brisk voice, swiveling the wheelchair toward me, "Norm here is our number-one porter." I snuck a glance at Norm, who glared back. "He hasn't lost a patient yet!" She laughed like we were all having tons of fun. "Hop in! No breaking the speed limit, Norm!"

I climbed into the wheelchair, feeling awkward and ridiculous. I can walk perfectly well, Nina. Let me tell you, I can definitely walk better than Norm. I could have *run* to the scanner, up and down the stairs, down the halls. But I guess traveling by wheelchair is some sort of hospital law, so I got in. I didn't want trouble.

We went so slowly it was unbelievable. Honestly, what if I was a *real* emergency, bleeding and everything? At one point, an old lady pushing a walker whisked right past us. We were going just the *teensiest* bit faster than the people standing completely still. I slid my feet off the footrests and scuffled them on the ground, trying to help us pick up some speed.

"Feet on the *rests*, please," Norm barked.

We inched our way into a greenish-blue elevator, then down a greenish-blue hallway into a department called Nuclear Medicine.

That name alone scared the pants off me, Nina. Not just *medicine* (which is bad enough), but *nuclear* medicine. My heart started pounding. My mind started racing. *Nuclear bomb...nuclear disaster...nuclear waste.* Think about it. Anything nuclear is *always* bad news. Actually, let me correct that. It's not just *bad* news, it's *disaster* news.

Dad was in the waiting room. He jumped up as we gradually slid in.

"Hey, Pumpkin!" he said. "I went to Emerg, but they told me you'd already left. That was *ages* ago! Where have you—" He stopped when I rolled my eyes and tilted my head back at the porter behind me. I could see on Dad's face the moment he understood. His mouth opened, his eyes got bigger, his eyebrows rose. Both my parents are so *obvious*. You can actually *see* what they're thinking most of the time. You can predict what they're going to say before they say it. Almost always.

Not me. Dad says I'll be a good poker player someday, because my face doesn't give anything away. Which is good. If I'm scared or upset it's nice that the whole world doesn't have to know it. But it gets me into trouble sometimes too. Mrs. D. always seems to think I don't apply myself (which I *do*), and Coach never thinks I'm trying hard at practice (which I *am*). The problem with Coach is that he doesn't think you're trying unless you're panting and yelling and grimacing and flailing and *showing* how hard you're trying. That's not me.

And the problem with Mrs. D. is sort of similar: unless you're catching her eye, smiling and hyper-nodding at everything she says, she thinks you're slacking off. You've probably never thought of this, Nina. You have the opposite of a poker face, a nice, smiley nonpoker face. But believe me, you get misunderstood if you have one.

"*Anyway*, you made it, ha, ha! That's all that matters, ha, ha!" Dad said. The sullen porter ignored him, practically dumped me out of the wheelchair into a real chair, shoved my chart across the counter at the clerk and left in huffy slow motion. The clerk glanced up, and Dad bounded over to her.

"Kasey Morgan is here for her bone scan," he said, dropping his voice at the last two words as though they were a private, terrible tragedy. Thankfully, the nuclear ladies were all very matter-of-fact and calm. A whole department of poker faces. I fit right in.

Turns out a bone scan has three parts, Nina:

1) A pinching, stinging injection of "radioactive dye" (I'm not joking—almost exactly like Spider-Man experienced, I believe);
2) More sitting around waiting and getting anxious;
3) The scan itself.

The needle hurt a ton. I didn't watch. Trust me—it's better not to watch. Whether it's nuclear stuff going in or blood coming out, it's *way* better not to watch. I dug my nails into my free hand and turned my head and studied a picture that was hanging on the wall. It was a photo of a young dad holding his baby who was just about to get a needle. Only, the baby didn't know what was coming, and the dad did. The baby was smiling in an interested way at that shiny, pointy thing, and the dad was looking away, his face scrunched up, wincing horribly like *he* was in pain, like *he* was the one getting the needle. I glanced over at my dad while the needle was pumping me full of nuclear substances, and he had the same expression as the dad in the picture!

The nuclear-needle lady seemed very relieved I wasn't a screamer. She said that even some adults are screamers and fainters when it comes to needles, but I was "amazingly calm." You can tell people that one, Nina. You don't need to mention that I was tasting blood from biting my cheek as the needle was searing its way into me.

After the needle, it was disappointing to discover that the radioactive stuff didn't make me glow in the dark like people do in the movies (not even a very faint, greenish shimmer around the teeth). It also didn't, for instance, give me the ability to climb walls. It's not like I tried in the bathroom or anything (which would be silly and germy as well, unless you really scrubbed your hands afterward), but I'm pretty sure. All that pain for nothing.

So now we sit and wait for the scan. Thank goodness that first clerk gave me this pad of paper and a pen so I can write to you, or I really would go out of my mind. Dad and I talked a little, but then we ran out of things to say. The magazines are hundreds of years old and pulsing with diseases and nuclear waste, no doubt. So I'm not touching those. The TV is blaring some stupid talk show, where the hosts scream-laugh and shout over each other in a fake friendly yet competitive way. Everything, apparently, is *shriekingly* funny. I am using all my poker-faced concentration to block them out.

Dad doesn't seem fussed by this germy hospital, Nina. Not at all. He touches *everything*. It's almost as if he makes a *point* of touching everything just to annoy me. Magazines, walls, the nursing desk, the *underside of his chair*. Seriously, I half expect him to actually lick something. Or try out a somersault, just so he can sample the floor germs. And then he pulls out a pack of gum, puts his hands all over it while opening it and offers me a piece! As if, Dad. As if.

I have to go. The clerk just dropped a hospital gown in my lap and told me "everything off but undies, honey!" Right out loud like that, in front of my dad and an old man sitting in the corner. Honestly.

⁓

I scrambled into the little cubicle to change. It only had a curtain as a door, and no amount of pulling that thing from side to side could close the gaps. First the stretcher paper, then the curtain…does nobody measure these things? So much for dignity and privacy.

The hospital gown shook my poker face, Nina. It was *hideous. Gown!* What a word to use for a dreary sack of worn-out cotton. It was more like a sheet—*huge* and faded hospital greenish blue, just like everything else. I swear, it was like a hospital invisibility cloak. I blended right in with the walls. I could probably have escaped except someone might have noticed my head and sandals zipping down the halls.

But worse, far worse—the gown only had *two* ties, at the back! And one was broken.

Help!

This is not how I wanted to face a scan of my bones.

Your slightly radioactive friend,
Kasey

Three

Dear Nina,

Scanned.

It was a weird experience, but at least it didn't hurt.

The room was huge and dark, like some freaky science-fiction movie set. The gigantic, circular bone-scanning machine sat right in the middle of the room, making a low humming noise. The machine had a bunch of scurrying attendants. One of them tried to make small talk with me. "How old are you? What grade are you in? What school do you go to?" The things adults always ask. Why, I wonder, don't they ask something honest, like "So, how do you feel about being fed into this nuclear monster we got here?"

I had to lie down on a stretcher by the machine's mouth. Thankfully, there was more of that incredibly thin, too-narrow sheet paper protecting me from the germs, diseases and leaked radiation of all the thousands of people who had been scanned before me. I'm being sarcastic, Nina. I'm letting you know because in writing it's hard to tell.

It was so *chilly* in that room. When I asked, I was told the machine likes it that way, and what the machine wants, the machine gets, apparently. I was absolutely shivering in my hideous hospital gown with the one tie missing on the back. Then one of the machine people said, "Oh, you're cold" and went and got a blanket for me. A *warm* one! They have this magical cupboard in the scanner room that keeps blankets toasty warm as if they've just come out of the *oven*. The machine person tucked it right around me like a mom at bedtime (which made me feel tearful, but I blinked hard).

It was heavenly to feel heat rather than radiation soaking into my shivering body. I somehow felt less afraid. Comforted. It truly is amazing what a blanket can do. It was one of the nicest things anyone ever did for me. I think every home should have a blanket-warming cupboard. And apparently, the machine couldn't care less whether you're under a blanket or not, which made me wonder why I had to be in the gown, but whatever.

The bone-scanner people kept telling me how *safe* it all was, how they did this a *million* times a day. But then how come Dad couldn't come in with me? And let me tell you, Nina, when that machine started to rev up, all the people in the room scrambled into a separate little room pretty quick and slammed the door shut! Which, of course, made me think they were lying about the safety thing. It was just me versus the nuclear scanning machine. It was a lonely feeling.

The scanner people watched through a window and talked to me over an intercom. Only it wasn't the "Can Tanner Zapetti please come to the office" kind of announcement we usually get at school. (Is he still destroying things, by the way? Write back, Nina. Please. You know things are weird when I'm even missing Tanner Zapetti.)

They were bone-scan-related announcements like "Stay still," "Now the machine will scan your legs," and "Breathe normally."

I've discovered that when someone *tells* you to breathe normally, it's very hard to do. In and out, in and out—you start to *notice* your breathing, coming in through your nose and mouth and filling you up, and the rise and fall of your ribs, and as you notice it, it doesn't seem normal at all. It speeds right up, and then you sort of try to slow it down, and you worry because none of it feels normal anymore. Breathing isn't something you should think about, because once you do, you ruin it. Anyway, I hoped the machine couldn't sense my totally abnormal breathing. Because what then? I wondered. Would it spit me out?

I closed my eyes tight during the scan and tried not to panic as the machine swooped around me, scanning all my bones from every possible angle. I could tell when it was close to my face because behind my eyelids it got darker. When the machine lost interest in my head and moved on, it got lighter.

And I tried not to imagine how to the machine I must look like a little skeleton lying there. That was an upsetting thought. All my little skeleton bones lying there, especially the skull—my *skull*—with those grinning teeth and eye holes and no real *nose*. All the parts that really make us who we are, the parts that we look at every day, like hair and eyes and skin and noses, stripped away, leaving just the bare bones.

I searched around in my mind for something else to think about. The skull thought reminded me of last Halloween because Kyle went as a little skeleton—very cute and not in the least bit creepy, although he thought he was. Remember he kept making that *kack!* sound he thought a skeleton, given vocal cords, would make? Anyway, that distracted me. It seemed very important, with my eyes squeezed shut inside that big machine in *June*, to remember what costume everybody wore last Halloween. Lots of zombies. We had a good time dressing as each other, hey, Nina? Nobody got it, so we had to put those nametags on, but I guess that's the price of a costume you don't buy at the store.

Lizzy as "the yard" was hilarious. Remember? She wore a poncho of fake grass, and she and Mom glue-gunned fake flowers and plastic toys onto it. And she had that felt potted shrub as a hat! My sister just doesn't care what anybody thinks.

Anyway, last Halloween got me to the end of the scan.

Then all the cowardly nuclear people came out of the safe little room they'd been hiding in, the lights brightened, and there seemed to be a general feeling of relief that the scan was over. The second I stood up, they were crumpling up the paper with my germs on it and smoothing out new paper for the next victim.

"Done," I said to Dad as the nurse walked me back into the waiting room. I snatched up my clothes from the little locker I'd left them in and escaped into the change room with the annoying curtain.

But you know what, Nina?

I wasn't done.

Your friend, who has a bad feeling about all this,
Kasey

Four

Dear Nina,

As we drove out of the city, Dad said we were supposed to go straight back to our little local hospital after the scan.

"Doctor's orders," Dad said with an apologetic tone in his voice.

We drove back to Ridgevalley in silence, except for when Dad pulled into a drive-through. I gave him my order, because it seemed silly not to get a burger and fries out of this whole ordeal. It wasn't Dad's fault, and he was being so nice.

Ridgevalley Hospital is so much smaller than the Royal Vic. *Way* smaller. I hadn't realized that until now. It actually looks quite peaceful. Until you get inside.

What is it about being inside a hospital that makes you feel sick? Or if not exactly sick, then helpless? I feel weaker here than I did at home yesterday, for example. Is it the horrible disease that may be devouring my very bones? Or is it just that I'm in the hospital and everyone's treating me like a patient? It's confusing. If you get treated like a weak hospital patient, you *feel* more weak-hospital-patient-ish, if you know what I mean. More scared and sorry for yourself.

I'm in a *new* hideous hospital gown (yay!), and I am wearing a plastic bracelet stating my name, my date of birth, my doctor's name and my patient number. Yes, I have a number, Nina. Not just 12, like on the back of my soccer jersey. Like a prisoner—number 348652. How hard to remember is that? Good thing it's bolted around my wrist. I am now sitting alone in a four-bed hospital room (number 212). I can hear Dad talking to the nurses down the hall at the desk. He's trying to get some answers about when I'll be able to go home.

Patient number 348652 is really, *really* hoping she doesn't have to spend the night here.

Think of it, Nina! *Night*, in the *hospital*. It's a very creepy thought. Nurses padding around in those soft shoes that nobody wears but nurses, sick patients coughing and moaning and lying in beds next to complete strangers, germs scuttling around because they never sleep, all the doors open, no locks... How could anyone ever feel safe enough to sleep? I can't decide whether it would be better to have another person in this room. On the one hand, I wouldn't feel so isolated. On the other, they might be a complete creeper or a cougher.

I really, really hope I don't have to be here overnight.

And if all that isn't enough to worry you, Nina, here's another thing. This hospital has lots of patients, but *there don't seem to be any children*. None. Well, one—me. But isn't that weird? I haven't seen one other child here. Only old people. I'm not just meaning adults, right? Really, really old people.

And you know how old people creep me out, Nina. I can't help it. The slowness. The teeth. The tendency to be super crabby. You would probably point out that I've never really known any really old people, and that I'm generalizing from that lady who runs the corner store and whose false teeth click and chatter almost independently of her mouth. I would then point to Norm the porter. He was a recent old person I've known, and he was miserable. So that's two.

Anyway, I'll let you know when I find out what is going on.

Oops. Nurse alert! Bustling into the room, pushing some rattling equipment.

Got to go.

To be continued.

~∽~

Have you noticed how I'm doing that little swirl thing? Like they do in books? It means that last part is over and time has passed, but I still have more to say before finishing this letter. WAY more.

Are you sitting down, Nina? Because it's bad news. You probably already figured that out. Nobody ever has to sit down for good news. I'm shaking as I write this, as you can possibly see. Where is a comforting warm blanket when you need one?

I have to stay here overnight. In the hospital. By myself. "Under observation" until a specialist has a look at my bone scan. Dad told me this with the nurse looking on. He sat on the bed and held my hand and told me very gently, with that wincing look like the dad in the picture where his baby was getting a needle. I didn't cry, and not only because the annoying nurse said brightly, "Kasey's a *big* girl. She's going to be a *brave* girl." Easy for her to say. She gets to get away from the creepy old folks and go back to her safe home tonight. No, I didn't cry because it was hard enough on Dad as it was, plus he has to go home and break it to Mom and the others. I put on my poker face and pretended to be very calm.

But I'll let you in on a secret, Nina. I don't feel very brave. Or calm. I'm just plain scared. Don't tell anybody.

To make sure I don't do a runner, the nurse hooked me up to a bodyguard named Ivy. She's a tall, pole-like machine on wheels with a liquid-bag face and long tube arms feeding into a needle that's taped right into the back of my hand (another big needle—didn't cry, but I can still taste blood from that raised lump where I keep biting the inside of my cheek). So Ivy and I are actually semipermanently attached, like Siamese twins. Technically, her name is IV, short for *intravenous* (I asked), which is apparently Latin for "into your vein." Latin always sounds so impressive, but it almost always seems to be just basic description. Anyway, I'm calling her Ivy, which is prettier and friendlier.

I'm going to need all the friends I can get here, Nina. Because not only do I have to spend the night here, pushing Ivy around, but when I asked the nurse where all the other kids are, she said there *are* no other kids in the hospital. None! The children's ward is closed for major renovations, so any serious emergency cases go into the city, and all other children (right now, only me— slow time for kids, apparently) are put in the "old folks' ward." So the good news is, I must not be a serious case. The bad news is that I'm in the geriatric ward. Old people, rooms and rooms of them, as far as you can see.

"So you see, Kasey, you're *special!*" said the nurse. "All the old dears will love having a child around." I smiled like I was supposed to. But behind my fake smile, I felt sick.

I'm not used to old people, Nina. My grand-parents aren't even old really. I mean, they're old*er*, but they still hike and travel and golf and email and everything. They actually tire us all out when we visit them. They're not like the old folks here. I don't know if you can even imagine how old some of the old people are here. Picture the oldest person you've ever seen or can even imagine. Then add a few years.

Now I'm feeling guilty and mean. Here I am, complaining that I have to spend one night in the hospital when most of these old folks look like they practically *live* here. They have pictures propped on the tables by their beds, and plants and flowers to make things more cheerful, but this seems to be their permanent *home*. How sad is that, Nina?

Maybe I can be useful cheering them up, even if I'm only here for one night. What do you talk about with super-old people? Health is out, obviously, because we're all in the hospital. Food? The weather? Mom says the weather is always a safe topic for just about any occasion. "Sunny out there, hey?" can lead into "Better than last June!" or "But the plants could sure use some rain." It's boring, but it's a start.

Dad has been trying to cheer *me* up.

"Nice big window," he said, looking down at the hospital workers throwing bags of I-hate-to-think-what into the big dumpsters below. "Natural light," he continued, tapping on the glass. He wasn't letting go of the wonders of the window. He was touching everything again—the windowsill, the wall, the back of the chair, the curtain around my bed. Anything that could hold or transfer germs.

"Here's the button for calling the nurses, Kasey. Right here. Give it a good long squeeze if you need them, okay? And ooh, gadget time! Let's see what your bed does!" He grabbed the remote. I braced myself, remembering how he recently broke our TV and took almost two weeks to assemble our swing set. First he raised and lowered the upper part of the bed, then the part under my legs, and then he crunched me up like a folding chair by raising both parts. "Cool!"

"Okay, okay, Dad," I said in a strangled voice (being crunched at the time). "Excellent bed demonstration. Now *stop*."

I was feeling tired, and my hand where Ivy's needle went into me was hurting in a pinchy, cold-liquidy way.

My dad looked concerned. He touched all the switches in the room, trying to turn off the overhead light, and gathered up a pile of grubby magazines to germ up my nightstand.

"After you wash your hands," I said, "you should just go home, Dad. I'll be fine." I gave this letter to Dad when he left. He's promised *not* to read it and to hand it *only to you*. We can trust him.

I'm sure I'll be home tomorrow, probably even back at school. Are we still doing end-of-the-year cleaning and watching movies? I love the end of June at school. There's an almost-summer-holidays slackness to it. A fun, no-rules feel in the air. I already miss it. I'm sure I'll be there tomorrow.

I just have to make it through this one night. One night won't be so bad. And it looks like I have this huge room at the end of the hall all to myself, although I have to stay in this bed and not try the other three. This is the only spot I'm allowed, apparently. I asked. The other beds are waiting for other patients, and they "don't want to have to make them again, missy." But really, after sharing a room with Lizzy and Molly for so long, for practically my whole *life*, and never, *ever* having any privacy, it seems very strange and even a little bit exciting that I'll be here on my own.

Well, not quite on my own.

Me and all the old people.

Wish me luck,
Kasey

Five

Dear Nina,

It's two o'clock in the morning of the longest night I've ever spent wishing for the morning to come. And that includes every Christmas Eve and the night after we watched part of that horror movie when I slept over at your house. Why did I ever let you convince me to do that when I'm a total chicken? Do you still think about that movie? I do. I'm definitely thinking about it right now, when I am alone and unprotected. Even though I tell myself to stop it, I keep thinking of clown puppets with evil red eyes and pointy fangs slinking down the hospital halls in the gloom...

So anyway (she writes nervously, trying to find something else to focus on), I know it is 2:00 AM because I have a loudly ticking, glow-in-the-dark clock on the wall in my room. Technically, it's 0200 hours, because the hospital doesn't use normal regular time. It uses *army* time, where all possible time is divided into twenty-four hours. So there's no 2:00 AM and 2:00 PM, there's 0200 hours and 1400 hours. It seems confusing and unnecessary until you think how a hospital runs all day *and* all night. So say some nurse says, "Give that patient his super-important, life-saving medicine at 4!" and leaves. The nurse who's left holding the medicine might think, "Wait a second...did she mean 4 AM or 4 PM?" and might make a mistake. A *life-ending* mistake. Or think of operations—you have to be *very* precise in situations where knives and anesthetics are involved.

So you start at midnight, which is 0000 hours (which I think is *hilarious*! Absolutely zero hours—none at all!), and after that everything goes pretty much according to regular numbers. For example, breakfast is at 7:00 AM (0700 hours), and school starts at 8:30 AM (0830 hours). But only until noon (1200 hours), when every hour after that is counted up from twelve. So 1:00 PM is 1300 hours, 2:00 PM is 1400 hours, 3:00 PM is 1500 hours, etc. until 11:00 PM (2300 hours).

Is this boring? I'm sorry if you're bored. I don't actually find it super interesting either. I'm just trying to erase the red-eyed clown puppets from my brain so I can go to sleep again. Writing to you helps.

I didn't figure out the clock thing all by myself. I asked Edna, the lady who came by to empty the garbage cans, and she sat right down on the bed and explained it all to me, which I thought was really nice of her. Other than Edna and the nurse who came in to check on Ivy and tell me that Mom had called, the only other person who's come into my room since Dad left was a completely silent, thin little person (I call her the Shadow) who brought me "dinner."

I say "dinner" in quotation marks because I suppose that's technically the meal usually served around 1700 hours (I'm such a show-off). I was starving, but "dinner" was *disgusting*. Horrible. How else can I describe it? Grim? Repulsive? Revolting? *Putrid*? Yes, putrid should definitely be in there somewhere.

I always thought being served food on a tray would be wonderful. Glamorous, even. Especially if you're lounging in bed! That seems like the life of someone rich and famous, right? Like a movie star. I always loved the idea of plates that you have to uncover, peering underneath while exclaiming, "Well, well, what have we here?"

So you can imagine my disappointment when I lifted the dull-pink plastic lid (not shining silver, like it should have been) off the main meal to reveal pieces of meat-ish substance floating in a greasy pool of cream sauce with some mushrooms perched evilly on top. *You* know how I practically have a phobia about mushrooms, Nina. I've told you my theory that they will eventually poison the whole human race. So I obviously wasn't eating any of *them*. I gagged just *looking* at them.

The smell of that main course almost knocked me out completely, but I gritted my teeth and ate a tablespoon of rice that hadn't touched the mush-rooms or been mucked up by the sauce. Then I covered that dish up super quick, because my stomach was *lurching* from the smell. There was a small foil-covered milk. I hate milk anyway, but especially when it's almost warm and supposed to wash down a vile-smelling dinner. There was a small cup of "fruit," which was really some canned sludgy, fruit-like cubes in syrupy water. I choked back what I think was a cube of peach. I even peeled the plastic off the cheese and nibbled a very little on that. It tasted like warm rubber. I ate the two crackers, trying not to touch them with my germy hands. I hadn't had time to wash them, because the Shadow just silently put the tray down on my table and wheeled the table right over top of me, pinning me to my bed.

I thought of that open bag of all-flavor jelly beans we had at home. You know how you take a scoop and pick out the best flavors, like the cherry ones, the limes and the lemons? And then there comes a time when the best flavors are all gone, because everyone likes those, so the next time you take a scoop you take the second-best flavors (maybe the peach or the licorice)? Then those are gone, so you eat the ones you really don't like at all, like the ones that are supposed to taste like pears or watermelon (but don't), just because you want some candy. I would have eaten every least-favorite jelly bean in the bag at this point. I was that hungry.

Ivy has made things less lonely. She's quiet, of course, but her blinking lights are cheerful, and she does this comforting drip-drip-drip of medicine water that is soothing and even mesmerizing if you're terrified and awake at, say, 0223 hours. And this may sound strange, but she's a good listener. Thoughtful. Considerate. She never interrupts And another bonus is that if I had to protect myself, I could swing her steel pole hard and really smack someone a good one. Right at the knees, I'm thinking. Anyway, she's happy, in her quiet way, to be useful.

She does, however, have to come everywhere with me, and I mean *everywhere*. For example, the washroom. I've gone once, and I don't think I'll be doing that again anytime soon. I left it for as long as I could, and I had to pull on my socks with just my right hand, which is awkward, but I'm scared to use my left hand because what if that needle gets banged around and slips into something that is *not a vein*? What then? Anyway, it took forever, but like I was going to walk into a hospital bathroom in *bare feet*. Can you even imagine the germs? Billions of them. Then I had to hold the back of my gown together with my right hand (I was walking right past the window) and push Ivy with my left. We clattered over to the washroom, and I had a moment of heart-stopping panic when it looked like she might not fit in the room.

"Okay, Ivy, just sort of...bend," I muttered, clanking her against the top of the door frame.

She did her best, but I had to tilt her so her liquid-bag head swung back and forth. After a lot of shifting and tugging, we were in.

The toilet is freakishly high, but I promise that's all I'm going to say about that even though I wonder *why* it's so tall. Believe it or not, there are some things I will not write about. But I will say that it is very, very difficult to give your hands a good scrubbing with lots of soap in the sink when one of them has a needle and a tube sticking out the back of it.

I wrestled Ivy out of the bathroom, making a loud racket in the quiet of the night, and when that noise died down, I heard another noise. What was that noise? I stopped and listened, my heart pounding. It was a strangled, gargling sound that made me feel cold right through.

I looked at the door to the room. It was propped wide open so nurses, hospital workers and murderous red-eyed clown puppets could slip in and out with ease. I pushed Ivy over warily, tightening my grip on her pole body. She's very graceful and silent on the smooth linoleum. We peeked out of the room and peered down the long hallway.

They dim the lights at night, so even though the hospital hallways are still lit, it's gloomy. Nobody was around. The noise was coming from up ahead on the right. As I got closer, it got louder. *Way* louder. A dreadful gasping, gulping, wheezing sound.

I swallowed and took a few silent footsteps down the hall. In my socks, I was just as quiet as Ivy.

I swear, Nina, a hospital at night is the loneliest place in the world.

I'd come to the doorway of the Ghastly Noise. It died down, then gathered, so that it was horribly loud, then sputtered out, then started up again. I pushed Ivy ahead of me with both hands and took a few steps into the room. Why did I do that, Nina? Why? In scary movies, the main character is always stupidly and frustratingly curious about that crashing/gurgling/cackling sound in the dark basement and just has to go and explore. And we always say or think, "Don't go! Stay where you are! Don't go into that dark room!" And here I was, creeping down a dim hospital hallway, turning in to a dark room to find out what an eerie, creepy noise was.

You're going to laugh, Nina.

Here I was, all freaked out, tense and sweating and ready to fight for my life, but it turns out the noise was just one of the old patients snoring! Snoring louder than I ever thought a human being (or any being) could snore, but still, *snoring*, with his mouth wide open. I wondered how he ever lived out in the normal, nonhospital world when he snores like that. How could his family stand it? How could anybody he lived with sleep through that racket?

I backed Ivy quickly out of the room, feeling guilty. I'd been worrying about hospital creepers, and it turns out the creeper was me! It isn't right for people who don't know you to see you when you're sleeping. I'd sure hate it if anybody watched me while I was asleep.

Thankfully, the nurse who'd checked on Ivy earlier came out of a room up ahead and walked quickly down the hall away from me to the desk. She didn't look my way, but I watched her wide, swaying back until she disappeared. So I wasn't the only person awake in the world! There was somebody here, somebody in charge. I pushed Ivy back to bed, huddled under the covers and grabbed the little remote with the nurse call button. I didn't press it, but holding it in my hand made me feel better.

And I wrote this letter to you. Thanks for helping me through The Night That Wouldn't End, Nina.

See you tomorrow.

Your friend who may or may not get some sleep,
Kasey
At 0322 hours (3:22 AM to all you nonhospital types)

Six

Dear Nina,

Hospitals wake very, very early. And they wake noisy, like my baby brother.

There are carts rattling, people talking loudly in the halls, patients coughing and calling out, bells ringing, you name it—all before 0700 hours. A new nurse came in to change Ivy's bag head and chattered away cheerfully at my barely awake self. I was, however, relieved to see that she was wearing plastic gloves. Finally (I thought), somebody who cares about cleanliness! Only, this nurse bustled in and out of the bathroom (touching the door every time) and came back to my bed and touched all over Ivy's tubes and bag. So it seems the gloves were for her own germ protection, not mine.

People just walk in and out of this room whenever they feel like it, Nina. There is no polite knock, no privacy. For example, a man walked straight in, said "good morning," slapped a breakfast tray on my table, raised the head of my bed and swung the table in front of me. I guess The Shadow only does dinners.

Each tray has a room and bed number on it, so that we all get the delicious food we crave, apparently. I'm the body attached to tray 212(2). After last night's dinner, I was actually afraid of breakfast. I lifted the lid very slowly, like I was disabling a bomb. Turns out it was only mucky oatmeal with a hard bun. I was nibbling a few bun crumbs and struggling to open the little foil-covered apple juice when Dad walked in.

"Morning, Pumpkin," he said cheerfully. But his eyes were worried. "How's my best hospital gal? I came as soon as I could. Hope you had a good night?"

"It was terrible. I'm starving," I said. So much for trying to be brave. Or subtle. It did the trick, though, because he went right down to the hospital coffee shop and brought back a hot chocolate, a huge blueberry muffin and a donut. And while I was ripping those apart like a starving wild animal, he gave me your note.

Thank you for writing back, Nina! Even if it was only a few sentences while my dad was standing there talking to your parents, and even though I'll probably be home today anyway. Seven exclamation marks!!!!!!! You're such a great friend!!!!!!!! (you deserve eight). It means so much to me to know that *you* know how much all this sucks.

⁓

I'm back.

Where do I begin? When Mom and the baby came in? Or when the group of doctors came in while they were here? Yes, maybe there. At 0824 hours (8:24 AM).

Even though a whole bunch of doctors swooped into my room (without knocking) like a flock of rumpled white birds, it was quite clear that only one of them mattered. The head doctor. He's a little guy with about six strands of hair pasted across his bald head that weren't fooling anybody. The others were just doctors in training, not yet really doctors, and while they politely gathered around and peered at the red lump on my ankle, they didn't dare say anything. The little guy—Dr. Roberts, or, as I call him, Dr. Robot (because that's exactly what he sounds like)— called the shots, no hospital pun intended.

So, after a bit of awkward, robotic small talk, Dr. Robot focused his laser-beam eyes on me.

Dr. Robot: Young lady. This bruise on your ankle. How did you get it?

Me: Playing soccer.

Dr. Robot (with a very thin little smile): Soccer. Well, I hope you won the game.

[Hysterical laughter from all the student doctors. I guess that was Dr. Robot's idea of a joke. And when Dr. Robot makes a joke, you'd better laugh, apparently. I could tell he didn't really care how the game ended, so I didn't tell him we actually lost 3–2.]

Dr. Robot: But seriously. It is clear from the bone scan that this red lump [he pointed with a pen at my leg, like he didn't want to touch it with his finger] indicates a bone disease called [osteo-something-something-itis. [I can't remember *everything*, Nina.It was a long, scary-sounding word. No matter what it's called, isn't it enough that it's a *disease of the bone*??]

Mom: A disease!

Dr. Robot: ...in which bacteria invade and devour the marrow of the bone.

[I was very proud of Mom for not saying, "The *marrow!*" or "The *bone!*" I think we were both stunned silent by those two cheerful words, *invade* and *devour.*]

Mom: So what do we—how can we cure it, Doctor?

Dr. Robot: Well, of course she has to go on a lengthy course of antibiotics. Many years ago, you wouldn't have been walking out of this hospital on two legs, young lady. [Uncertain laughter among the student doctors, quickly stopped as Dr. Robot whirled around at them]. Yes? Yes? Who here thinks the amputation of limbs is some big joke??

Me and Mom (shrieking at the same time): *AMPUTATION*???

[Really, Nina, wouldn't *you* have shrieked that word?]

Dr. Robot: At *one time*, very possibly. Historically. Not *now*, of course. Now listen to me. [He spoke in an irritated way and slowed down like he was talking to small children.] The treatment is a course of antibiotics for four to five weeks.

Mom: So pills, then?

Dr. Robot: IV antibiotics and antimicrobial therapy, Mrs. Morgan. High doses of intravenous drugs administered by professionals. Bottom line, we'll need her here in the hospital for at least a month.

Did you read to the end of that, Nina? I wouldn't blame you if you were sort of skimming. I do tend to go on and on. But that last sentence is important, wouldn't you say? In case you didn't catch it, quick summary: **I WILL BE IN THIS HOSPITAL, HOOKED UP TO IVY, FOR**

AT LEAST A MONTH!!!!!!! Now *that* deserves at least seven exclamation marks.

A month at *least*. Possibly even *longer*. I'm still in a state of shock at this news. A small red lump on my leg, and *poof!* There goes half of summer vacation. July. In the hospital. I can barely take it in. All those lonely nights, all the small, darkish hours, alone here in room 212. Or, possibly worse, with a roommate. All the endless days with the old people. How will I ever live through this?

I have to tell you, Nina. I did not take this news very well. But at least the doctors had all swarmed out of the room before I started to cry. Don't tell anyone.

Mom grabbed my hand and said, "It's okay, Kasey. It's going to be okay—we'll get through it," and then ruined it by starting to cry too. The baby woke up and started to cry. It was ridiculous, all three of us sitting there sniveling together.

A big redheaded nurse walked by the open doorway and paused. She did a thoughtful little double knock before she came in.

"Oh dear, oh dear," she said, looking from me to Mom. "What's the catastrophe?"

Good word. It felt like a catastrophe. Actually, it felt like a CATASTROPHE.

"Well," Mom sniffed, wiping her eyes with her hand. "We've just had some terrible news. Kasey here is going to have to be in the hospital for a *month*."

I tried to blot my nose with a sheet from my bed.

The redheaded nurse took this staggering news calmly.

"Yes, I heard. That's not great, is it, Kasey? In fact, it sucks. *But* I've had a word with Dr. Roberts, and there's no reason you shouldn't be completely cured after that! That's the *good* news, right? You'll be all better."

"Yes," I whispered, because I had to. It *was* the good news in the whole thing. But it kind of sat alone and cold and forgotten in the huge, dark shadow of the bad news.

"So," said the redheaded nurse, "we just have to be practical and find ways to make your month here the best it can possibly be." She smiled and plopped down on the bed beside me. She was a very big lady, with a round face and small blue eyes that creased up when she smiled.

"Think of this room as Camp Kasey." She didn't say it in a babyish way. Just in a bright, matter-of-fact way. "What would make it fun? Some of your own stuff?" I thought about it, then nodded. It *would* make a difference if I had my books and stuffies and drawing stuff.

"How about your own nightgown? Glamorous as these may be," she said, tugging a little on the sleeve of the hospital gown I was wearing, "they're a bit drafty out back." I gave a snorty, watery giggle.

"Yeah, I hate them. And I need my slippers," I said. "For the germy floor. And my robe."

"Excellent! That's a great start. Mom, can we bring Kasey some of her own stuff?"

"Absolutely," Mom said, nodding and jogging the baby on her hip. He was grinning and batting at Ivy, gripping her tubes in his fat little fist.

"So there's no Wi-Fi or even cable in this part of the hospital, in case you were wondering. The old folks don't miss them. But we do have TVs for rent! They're old too, and only get two channels, but still, better than nothing. Do you want me to call the guy for you?" Mom and I both nodded, and the nurse bustled out.

"Well, good," Mom said as she bounced the baby gently on the bed. His fat legs buckled underneath him as he grinned and lurched, smiling up at Ivy. "This is good. At least we have a bit of a plan, hey, Kasey? I'll pack up your favorite things, and we'll visit a lot…" Her voice trickled off.

I said nothing, fighting back tears again. I cuddled with the baby until I had myself under control.

Then he started fussing, and Mom said he was hungry and she better go.

"You okay?" she whispered.

"Yeah," I said, even though I wasn't.

"You better get some rest and get better, Pumpkin."

Get better. I was sick. *Diseased*, in fact. And I couldn't even feel it.

When Mom and the baby left, I wondered what I was supposed to do all day. What do you do in a hospital all day long? I glanced out the window and watched a loud garbage truck do a beep-beeping reverse up to the dumpsters. I looked at the germy pile of magazines on my nightstand and even considered opening one. I watched the clock on the wall: 0945 hours.

I lay back and closed my eyes, which were tearing up babyishly again.

It's 9:45 AM on the first day of my month in the hospital.

Your friend (who is still in shock),
Kasey

Seven

Dear Nina,

The nice nurse is named Rosie, which exactly suits her because she's big and has red hair. Your name suits you too, Nina. It's fun and a little different and suits your wild, curly black hair. I think Kasey suits me too. Katherine-Charlotte, as I've mentioned, is not me at all. Think Katherine-Charlotte and you immediately think of a girl in a dress, right? Possibly even a bonnet. Have you ever seen me in a dress, Nina? The hospital *gown* doesn't count.

Did you know my sister Lizzy is really Elizabeth-Grace? Truth. Now, *you* know Lizzy.

Could you ever call her Elizabeth-Grace without bursting out laughing? My parents learned their lesson with Lizzy and me—they didn't pass on the curse of the hyphen to the other three.

Anyway, Rosie saw me staring in a hopeless way at the clock and asked me whether I would like to go on a tour of the ward. It wasn't like I had a lot of other entertainment options, so I said okay. She found a hospital robe to cover up the back of me. It is faded hospital blue and as big as the school field, so she had to do a bunch of wrapping and tying and hiking upping. Finally, when I was all bundled up and looking like I was going to some bizarre martial-arts contest, we set out to be stared at by strange and sick old people.

"So we'll show you around your new home away from home, get you more settled feeling," Rosie said. "The geriatric ward is really a comforting, reassuring place."

It wasn't. Just letting you know right now that it wasn't.

We started at the front desk, which is the control center of the unit. It's what you might expect—

computers, binders, phones, paper, flowers in vases, a few cards propped up. It's where visitors can go to ask which room the person they're visiting is in. The unit clerk, who's the control freak for the unit, is a busy woman who kept standing up and then bouncing down heavily in her chair. Her name tag said *Barbara*, but privately I call her the Bouncer. She let me do a test of the intercom, barking instructions at me like really only she could know how to use that thing. She and Rosie thought I'd be all nervous, but I grabbed the intercom and said, "Testing, one, two, three. This is only a test," clear as a bell. They didn't know that we do office duty at school, Nina, so intercoms are nothing new.

Then Rosie introduced me to the row of old people in wheelchairs who were sitting by the front desk.

"This is Edward," she said. A very thin old man glared at me from under bushy gray eyebrows. But in fairness, he seemed to have a sort of perma-glare. He kept glaring after he looked away from me.

"And this is Yolanda and Sadie, who are having their little nap. And *here* we have our oldest resident, ninety-four years young, little Missy Wong! Hello, little Missy," Rosie said in a loud voice.

Missy Wong was a tiny woman, smaller than *me*, whose thin white hair was scraped up into two pigtails on the top of her head and tied with pink ribbons like a two-year-old girl's. I wondered if she *wanted* her hair like that or if the nurses just thought it looked cute. She turned her flat, round, wrinkled face toward me and smiled. She had sparkling little dark eyes and a teeny bump of a nose and *no teeth at all!* None. Just gums. A gummy, toothless smile. I was not expecting that at all, and I'll be honest, Nina, no teeth at all is quite a shocking look.

I took a step back, but she grabbed my hand with both her thin little hands and held on tight, smiling and nodding at me, and pulling me down into the chair beside her.

"She likes you, Kasey!" Rosie said. "She's such a sweetie. She's pretty hard of hearing and doesn't talk at all, so we don't really know how much she remembers, but we still communicate just fine." Rosie smiled at Missy Wong and pointed at me, and Missy Wong smiled and nodded and tightened her grip on my hand, and I smiled and nodded and started to wonder if this smiling and nodding would go on forever and when it would be rude to stop.

"Twenty-one's calling, Rosie," barked the Bouncer. "Again. One thing after another with him."

"Be right there." Rosie turned to me and Missy Wong. "I'll just answer this call while you two get acquainted."

I was left holding hands with a little ninety-four-year-old I'd just met. I'm ashamed to say I panicked a little, Nina. I racked my brain for something to talk about.

"Have you had your breakfast?" I asked, miming eating with an imaginary spoon. She smiled and nodded, but I wasn't sure if it was about the breakfast, because the nod kept on going.

"I like your hair," I said, pointing at my head, then at hers with my Ivy-tubed hand. She still had a firm grip on my other one, and she kept nodding, as though she was thinking of something else.

Suddenly she pointed my hand at a shawl she had wrapped around her. It was all rumpled and slumped down, and she struggled to pull it up, so I helped. As we yanked away at the shawl, I was shocked to discover that Missy Wong was strapped into her wheelchair with a seat belt. A seat belt, Nina! Right across her lap, like she was in a car, not in a stopped wheelchair. I looked down the row at the others. Same thing. I felt sad and angry for these old people, forced to sit or sleep sitting up here at the front desk without being able to get up and walk away when they wanted to.

We finally worked the shawl up around her tiny shoulders, which seemed to make Missy Wong happy. It was a beautiful shawl—black and silky with a long fringe and embroidered in brilliant rainbow colors. A peacock spread his gorgeous feathers and strutted in front of an old temple, masses of flowers led to a silvery-blue river framed by cliffs and trees, and people in triangle hats worked in fields shimmery with water. Elegant birds stretched their long wings in the background, and a fiery-red dragon wound his scaly body around a tower in a sky studded with stars. Missy Wong traced my hand over each scene like she was telling me a story. Maybe she was.

"Beautiful!" I said, smiling and nodding. "It's a beautiful shawl." And it was. I was glad she had something beautiful, something that wasn't hospital blue, something from her life before she came here. She hunched happily into the shawl, smiling and wrapping it around her. Then her face got kind of sneaky, and she pointed my hand down at the dragon on her shawl, then over at the desk, where the Bouncer was bellowing into the phone about some supplies that were late. Our eyes met for just a second, and even though I'm not sure, I think Missy Wong might understand more than people give her credit for.

"Sorry 'bout that." Rosie bustled back, her cheeks flushed. "How about we take Missy Wong on our tour? Would you like that, honey?" Rosie bent down, miming *vrooming* in a wheelchair. She's so nice, Nina. When you come to visit, I'll introduce you.

We went slowly down the hall. Missy Wong tapped her feet in their wooly pink slippers as we went, and with her pigtails bobbing and the fringe of her shawl swaying, I almost forgot she was wheelchair-walking—it looked more like she was dancing.

"Why are they all strapped in?" I whispered to Rosie.

"Oh, sorry, should have explained that," Rosie said. "It's for their own protection. Many of the old folks need help to walk, and if somebody's not right there when they get up, they might fall and break a hip or something." That made me feel a bit better.

We wandered through the unit, smiling and nodding at everyone we met. I've never seen such old people, Nina, and some of them seemed so sick. Some had tubes in their arms and even up their noses! Some were crying out, coughing or just lying there. The just-lying-there ones were the saddest of all. We got glimpses of them as we walked down the hall. But Rosie chattered away cheerfully, and she works there every day, so you must get used to it.

I saw the blanket warmer, the linen cabinets, utility room, storage room and staff room. Rosie pulled out a plastic container of soft caramels from a cabinet. The container had a *Rosie's Private Stash! Keep Out!* sign taped to the top, but she let me and Missy Wong each have one.

After the tour they dropped me at my room, and I watched them move slowly down the hall, Rosie's cheerful voice fading away.

I paced around my room, trying to calm down. Because, Nina, I felt panicky. My hands were freezing cold and my stomach was fluttery, the sort of feeling you get when there's a test you haven't studied for, or your team is playing the best team in the league. A pit-of-the-stomach feeling of dread mixed with fear mixed with worry.

If I had to put my feeling into one word, it would be *trapped*.

I could not imagine staying here for a whole month. How on earth was I supposed to get better in a whole unit of very sick people? I looked at the three empty beds in my room and imagined the sick and scary old people that might end up being my roommates.

I wanted to yank Ivy out of my arm and run and run and run away from all of these old, sick people. I closed my eyes and saw myself racing down the stairs, hospital robe flapping, through the doors and out into the sunshine. Running all the way home.

But I didn't, because I'm a big girl, a brave girl. I took a deep breath. I ran on the spot until I was sweating. I was shocked to find that it tired me right out. I crawled into bed, thinking I might have a little nap before I have to face whatever horror they'll be bringing for lunch.

Only 11:12 AM on my first day in the hospital, and I'm already living like an old person.

Please write or visit, Nina. Pleasepleaseplease pleaseplease*please*.

That sounds desperate, and I don't even care.

Your pathetic friend,
Kasey

Eight

Dear Nina,

Wow!!!!!!!! I can't believe you and your mom and Coach brought the whole team to visit! I guarantee that this hospital unit has never, ever had two vanloads of girls visit anyone. All the old folks are talking about it! Rosie tells me that even patients who almost never leave their rooms came to the door to see who was making all the noise. Not that you made a lot of noise—it's just *different* noise from hospital noise. The noise of giggling and movement and happiness and *life* rather than the buzzing, rattling, moaning and beeping sounds of a hospital. It was so wonderful to see you guys.

I never expected a visit from all the Wildcats. And straight from practice!

I can't thank you and your mom enough for the cookies. You guys must have baked all day! I've been wolfing cookies all evening. I put the box right beside me on my bed, within grabbing distance. The cookies are delicious and very effective at getting the taste of "dinner" out of my mouth.

It felt very lonely here after you left. It was so much fun, and then *poof!* It was over. Somehow this room seems emptier than it was. Quieter. I'm back to watching the clock. I'm thinking of counting out days like they do in prison movies, with a piece of chalk on the wall—four ticks, then a diagonal one straight through. Groups of five days. One month would be six groups of five days. Only six groups of five. When you break it down like that, it doesn't seem so bad, hey, Nina? I just need a piece of chalk.

It's 1830 hours. Six thirty. Still early. Lots of time for all the healthy kids to be outside playing, enjoying what looks like a beautiful day out there. I hope you're outside, Nina, running around with my brother and sisters. Keep an eye on them for me, okay?

Your inside, unhealthy friend,
Kasey

PS. That last letter I handed you may possibly be depressing. I'm sorry—I didn't have time to happy it up.

Another PS. Lydia and Jamie seemed disappointed I didn't have a cast. *Very* disappointed. They made me feel quite guilty about it, like I'm just pretending to be sick to get attention. Could you tell them that my leg bone is not broken but is merely being eaten from *inside me* by disgusting, ravenous bacteria? That ought to shut them up.

Yet another PS. Ivy is not "gross" and was slightly offended by the *eeeewwwws* of the team. She didn't say anything, but I could tell. She is a good companion, a defensive weapon in the middle of the night and a helpful feeder of the medicine I need to get better. You can tell anyone that.

One more PS. Missy Wong is not "that creepy, toothless old lady at the desk" as Shelby called her. Does that girl ever think before she speaks? Yes, Missy Wong is old. She is toothless. But she's not creepy. She can't help not speaking or being old. She was once a kid like us a long time ago, playing with other kids, running around. Oh, and the pigtails are *not* her fault. I asked. The nurses just think they look cute on her, and she seems to like them. Anyway, you can tell Shelby I'll visit her in eighty years, and we'll see how wonderful both of us are looking.

Very last PS. I seem crabbier when I PS, so maybe I won't in future letters.

Nine

Dear Nina,

Mom and the others brought some more of my stuff, so my corner of this huge room is starting to look as messy as home. I still shudder at the image of Molly cheerfully dragging a green garbage bag of my stuffies *along the hospital floor.* What is it with my family and germs?

Anyway, I have books! Books I have already read, but sometimes those are the best kind. I don't mind knowing what happens. I actually like that. Just looking at them makes me feel like I have friends here.

I also have some of my own clothes. But here's the problem, Nina—Ivy. She doesn't mean to be a problem, but because we're attached, I can't put my left arm into any sleeve! It would have to go all the way over Ivy's bag head, down her pole, maybe even over her *wheels*. It's impossible. This "gown" I'm wearing is different. It has three snaps along the shoulder area, because some smart hospital person thought at some point, Hey, what about those people with ivs? How the heck are they supposed to get in and out of this? I know—let's design a hideous gown that you can rip right off!

But while it is practical, I hate my hospital gown. I hate it with a desperation I haven't hated anything before in my life. I may have mentioned its ugliness before. And possibly its hugeness. Not to mention the draft at the back. So anyway, I was determined to wear my own cozy, closed-at-the-back nightgown and my purple fuzzy robe. But how?

I shut the door to my room and shoved a chair in front of it so nobody would barge right in while I was changing, which, believe me, they do.

I managed to get my hospital gown off (and gave it a good, strong, soccer kick into the corner). I struggled into my own nightgown, got as far as pulling it up, getting my right arm into it, and then I stopped, not knowing what to do with that left arm, the one joined to Ivy. I ended up tucking the useless nightgown-arm in, and just rocking a bare-arm-and-shoulder look. Toga style. Not really what I'm comfortable with, so I shrugged my robe over my shoulders and felt better. More normal and in control. Less *hospital patient*, if you know what I mean.

I slapped the pile of germy magazines down on one of the other nightstands, sanitized my hands and stacked my books and my drawing stuff on mine. I arranged my stuffies like I do at home, the best ones up near my head, the lesser stuffies under the blankets down at my feet. I put up the "get well" drawings Molly and Kyle drew for me on the small corkboard, which helped to cover up an ugly hospital notice on needle disposal.

Kyle drew a huge pile of dirt. Must've used an entire brown crayon. On top of the dirt he drew a spidery backhoe with a big open mouth saying, *NO dont eat drit!* which I'm sure is hilarious backhoe humor if you're nearly three. Molly drew an uncertainly smiling baldish person (which is supposed to be me, only I can't have that huge a head, can I?) with her arms, round hands and stick fingers all stretched out, saying, *My bones are feeling all of them FINE!* The word *fine* is underlined four times in red pen. She's determined that my bones will get better, so I will be too.

That's going to be my motto for this month, Nina. My bones are feeling all of them FINE!

So you know the ice-cream truck that comes around in the summer with that piercing song every kid seems to know in their bones means *ice cream*? And how if you're inside, you hear that song and freeze? Then you run out, wild-eyed, clutching the money Mom scrambled to find in her wallet, trying to figure out where exactly the truck is? And you start running. You run and listen and turn and run some more and finally you find it, and it stops, and you agonize about what to choose, and finally you just pick something. And Mom tells you that for that money you could buy a whole tub of ice cream, which is exactly *not* the point. The point is the excitement, the chase. The point is the whole idea of the truck.

Well, exciting news! The hospital has a sort of ice-cream truck, only it's a snack cart that comes around some evenings. I'm trying to figure out exactly which evenings so I can look forward to it. This evening was the first time I'd seen this wonderful thing.

I was lying in bed, clock-staring (1914 hours, 7:14 PM). The TV, by the way, is lame. Babyish kids' shows on one channel, and baseball (or worse, golf) on the other. Anyway, I heard a rattling sound pass my door. It stopped, then backed up.

"Wow, a *kid*!" said the girl pushing the cart, like I was a zoo exhibit. She rolled the cart into my room, right up to the side of my bed. It looked sort of like the regular food carts but appeared to have way better food. "What're you doing here?"

We both seemed astonished to see another person under the age of seventy.

"They say my leg's sick," I said.

"Sucks. No other kids in the whole place. But at least you got your own room. Look, you want some snacks?"

I hesitated. "Like, for free?" I asked.

I know, I know—I'm not sounding very smart here. Or cool. Fact is, though, I didn't happen to bring any money on this adventure, Nina. And how stupid would I have looked if I took a whole bunch of stuff and had no way to pay? I'd be washing the gross remains of other people's dinners off plastic plates, probably.

The girl gave a snort-laugh. "Absolutely free, kid." She saw me look hungrily at the sandwiches and chips and small packets of cookies.

"Look, take anything you want. I got a full load today, and the old folks will never eat it all. Leave some of the soft stuff though." She sat down on the side of my bed and started to chip blue nail polish off her thumbnail.

I took a sandwich and a bag of chips. She looked up, said, "Oh, *please*" and tossed me some cookies, a pudding cup, a granola bar and even a tiny chocolate bar. "Better stock up," she said. "The food they serve here sucks."

The snack girl talked to me while I gulped down that delicious food. Her name is Louise. Louise isn't like anyone we've ever met, Nina. She's got spiky black hair, smeary black eye makeup, ripped jeans and a black-and-red-checked shirt under her hospital apron, and she smells a little bit of smoke. She is in eleventh grade at the high school and *hates* it. She is a vegetarian. When she said this, I thought she said "veterinarian," which seemed strange, not only because this is a people hospital but because she's pretty young to be a doctor. After a really bizarre conversation where I asked her about sick animals and she talked about vegetables, we figured it all out. She asked me about my family and seemed envious of my sisters and brothers. Louise lives with just her mom, and I don't think they get along.

"Well, better get carting," she said, releasing the cart's brakes with a stamp of her black Converse. She turned at the door. "Hey, you know about the buzzer button? If you need the nurses, you just press that and they'll come. See you soon, kid."

She doesn't say "kid" in a mean way. Just in a casual way, like it's a nickname. I like it.

Like I said, I don't know what the cart's schedule is, but I'm feeling happier knowing that snacks and Louise are part of this hospital, even if it's only sometimes.

Anyway, I thought you should know about "The Incident of Louise and the Snack Cart." I'll try to get more information from her about why she hates high school. I know we'll only be going to junior high in September, but we should prepare ourselves, I think.

Your finally not-ravenous friend,
Kasey

Ten

Dear Nina,

Day five.

Only my fifth day in the hospital, but already it seems like I've been here forever. I can only vaguely remember my pre-hospital life. Okay, I'm exaggerating, but seriously, Nina, it feels like I've been here for a month already. I already have a routine (brace yourself, it's going to sound totally pathetic).

0730 hours: breakfast (I won't complain anymore about the food—that must be getting old.)
0745 hours: reading or clock-watching

0830 hours: sitting with the old folks at the desk, watching the Bouncer

0900 hours: taking Missy Wong for a walk around the ward

1000 hours: visit from Mom and the baby, then drawing/reading/clock-watching

1130 hours: lunch (more food I could complain about, but won't)

1200 hours: fast-walking around the unit or seeing if the nurses need any help (I helped distribute jugs of ice water today.)

Afternoon: clock-watching/reading/drawing/ writing letters to you/hoping it's a snack-cart day

1700 hours: dinner (see, no complaining)

Evening: pretty much the same as the afternoon

Writing all that down just depressed me more.

Anyway, my point is that something different happened this afternoon. Something not in my routine.

I was reading when a nurse I call the Grumbler came in.

"Bath time, Kasey!" she announced.

Bath time. Like I was two years old. Hey, let me just grab my foam letters, water toys and bubbles, and I'll meet you at the tub! Of course, I didn't actually say that. I often think things I don't say, which is probably a good thing. Anyway, I've obviously been washing in the bathroom (did I mention this was my fifth day here?) because I didn't know they even had showers. But apparently it's a bath.

"Where exactly do I have a bath?" I asked her carefully.

"Oh, tub's just down the hall," she said, plucking at Ivy's tubes. "Haven't you seen it? Got a winch and everything!"

A *winch*? Is that like the crane in Kyle's book? This did not make me feel very optimistic about bath time. In fact, I was starting to get a pit-of-the-stomach feeling of dread about it. I had a vivid mental picture of being lowered *naked,* in slow dips and lurches by a huge machine, into a big tub.

"You know what?" I babbled. "I've been doing a *great* job scrubbing myself down in my own bathroom. Even washed my hair just two days ago. I'm, in fact, *incredibly* clean."

The Grumbler wasn't even listening. She changed Ivy's bag head and then started pulling her to the door, so I pretty much had to follow her.

We went down the hall into a room I thought was a big storage closet. But, sure enough, there was a bathtub in there. The Grumbler was already turning on the water and swilling out the tub with her hand. Very effective, scientific disinfecting.

"You guys must be scrubbing this bathtub out with tons of disinfectant all the time, hey?" I asked nervously. She didn't even glance over. But they must, right? Right? I mean, all of these sick people...just imagine the germs! I can't even think about it.

The tub was huge and (of course) hospital green. No joke, Nina, my whole family could have fit in there at the same time. It also had very steep sides, like a ditch, like it was designed to keep people *in* and prevent them from scrambling *out*. There was a big dangling, strappy thing attached to the ceiling, linked to a machine over on the right.

"Yep, that's the winch, Kasey," the Grumbler said as she stood up, her face flushed from the hot water. "And let me tell you, that thing has saved our backs!" While the water ran, I had to listen to how they used to have to wrestle old people into that tub with two (and sometimes three) nurses. But now they strap them up to that winch, which does the job. Great, just great. So many people give you too much information.

"That's enough water," I said. "I'm just going to have a quick bath. *Really* quick. And I absolutely don't need any—uh—winching, thank you. So—you can, you know, leave." I tried to say that as politely as I could, but it still came out sounding sort of rude. Thankfully, the Grumbler isn't a sensitive type. She just asked whether I needed help with my clothes, told me not to get the hand attached to Ivy in the water, and plunked a little step stool in front of the least steep part of the tub so that I could climb in.

"I'll be back in a couple of minutes, Kasey," she said as she left, leaving the door not exactly open but not exactly closed either.

I waited a few seconds to make sure she was gone, then slammed the door and had the fastest, most awkward bath any human ever had. Seriously, bathing in a *puddle* would have been more dignified. Not being able to use my left arm was not ideal. Try shampooing your hair with only one hand. It feels weird and weak and exactly half as effective. Anyway, I was dressed, toweling my hair and calculating how many more times I would have to endure hospital bath time, when the Grumbler came back. She seemed very pleased that I didn't need anything in the way of work from her.

So here I lie, back in my bed, sort of bathed, sort of clean. I'm thinking that sink in my bathroom is looking extremely good bathwise.

Your semiclean friend,
Kasey

Eleven

Dear Nina,

It is 0210 hours (2:10 AM, the middle of the night, in case you haven't been reading my explanations about the time). At home, on New Year's Eve or if we were having a sleepover or something, I would have begged and pleaded with my parents to let me stay up past midnight. Here in the hospital, all I want is to be able to sleep the night away. Night is very, very long when you don't sleep. Think of it. It's like the whole day long—all that time we're up and going to school and playing soccer and eating and doing homework—but without the light and people and things that keep you busy.

So I'm writing to you. *Not* thinking about evil clown puppets at all.

My family came to visit yesterday evening, just after I finished that last letter to you. While Mom was trying to keep the baby from rolling off the bed and Dad was chasing Kyle around the room, Molly leaned over, put her hands on either side of my face and whispered very dramatically, "Kasey, how are your sick *bones*?"

I wanted to laugh, but she was so serious that I had to keep a straight face. I showed her the medicine dripping from Ivy's bag head into the tube leading into my arm. I tried to explain that it's kind of like Ivy and me are holding hands, only sort of with medicine (and a steel needle, and blood, but I didn't say that). Mom couldn't even look at the needle taped into my hand, but Molly was very interested and kept watching the tube and announcing, "There goes a *nudder* drip of med'cin. Nudder one. Nudder…"

"It's weird without you at home," Lizzy said in her slow way. "I used to think that it would be great to have more room, to only have to share with one other person, but I don't think that anymore." I knew exactly what she meant. Sometimes you wish for something without even really thinking about it. I've wished for my own room for so many years, and yet I would give anything to be back in our crowded room and hear Lizzy breathing beside me now. Or to hear Molly toss and turn and gasp and mutter in her sleep. It seems incredible that any of that ever annoyed me.

Kyle brought his favorite book to "read" to me. You guessed it. The truck one. I believe you have also read this "story" to him many times. There is really no story at all, just a bunch of oddly talkative trucks at a construction site, explaining in excruciating detail the technical, construction-related things they do. Wow, that is one boring book. Kyle doesn't let you cheat either. Remember the one part that goes on for a whole page where Dumpty the dump truck describes how he dumps stuff? Seriously, he— and why always *he*, incidentally? No *girl* trucks around?—just *dumps stuff*. That's it. He dumps stuff. But what could be a two-word explanation becomes an entire loooong page. So I always try to condense and skip ahead, but Kyle never lets me. I must say, he's pretty smart at identifying the different trucks and their functions. So am I after reading that book eight million times. Front-end loaders? Check. Scrapers? Check. Backhoes? I will never confuse them with, say, bulldozers. Dozer the bulldozer would be very disappointed in me if I did. So would Kyle.

Of course, the visit ended with the baby getting increasingly fussy and then starting to cry, and Kyle not listening when he was told a hundred times to *not* haul on the curtain around the bed, and Molly having to raise her voice to announce each drop of medicine. The usual Morgan-family chaos. Mom and Dad looked frazzled, so I told them they should probably head home.

What I really felt like saying, quite desperately, was "Please stay here, all of you, please just sleep in the extra three beds right here in this room. Don't leave me alone. I'm scared of the night." Lizzy understood, I think. She gave me a worried look and a tight hug.

"I'll bring in Squeakers when I can," she whispered into my shoulder during the hug. I laughed at that joke, imagining our crazy little dog barking and running down the hospital halls.

Before she left, Lizzy handed me a crumpled square of something in aluminum foil she dug out of her hoodie pocket.

Then there was a flurry of Morgans hugging and kissing and waving and leaving. And after they left, I felt very lonely, so I opened up Lizzy's gift.

It was a piece of lasagna.

I laughed at that—*you* would have laughed at that, Nina. Only Lizzy would think of bringing lasagna as a gift. Other people would talk themselves out of it because even though they know I love lasagna, they would think bringing it to the hospital would be messy or weird. So they would bring a stuffie or candy or something else nonleaky.

But that was the best piece of cold lasagna I ever ate with my bare hands. Sorry if I got lasagna prints on this letter.

Thanks for keeping me company during this endless night and listening to my lasagna stories.

Your slightly sleepy friend,
Kasey

Twelve

Dear Nina,

I have to tell you about a dream I had after I wrote to you last night.

In my dream, Ivy was a real person! A tall, thin, pale girl with a gentle smile and blue-green hair. Kind of like a shy, quiet girl who might sit at the back of the classroom. Only weirder. In the dream, we were good friends, like you and I are, Nina—almost sisters. And we weren't in the hospital. Ivy and I linked arms and walked through this sunny forest that had flowers blooming and peacocks strutting here and there, and it was all beautiful and happy.

Until it *wasn't*.

Because I began to feel afraid, for some reason, and I looked over at Ivy (this is making me scared even writing it in the sunny daytime), *and she was a fanged, red-eyed clown puppet!* I pulled away from her and tried to run, but I ran in that slow-motion, underwater speed you run in dreams. Ivy the clown puppet easily caught up with me and grabbed my arm in a tight, pinching grip that got more and more painful…

And then I woke up. Gasping and choking and muffled-shrieking and sweating like we'd just had soccer practice. I grabbed Ivy's cool pole body just to make sure it was her, and her bag head swayed in a normal, reassuring way.

And my hammering heart got quieter.

And I lay in my lonely room and watched the clock and Ivy's steady drip until morning finally came.

If you have any theories about that awful dream, I'd be glad to hear them.

Your friend (who gives you her word she will never morph into anyone else),
Kasey

Thirteen

Dear Nina,

Thank you for your letter!!! I could tell you were trying to make it seem like I'm not missing anything by being in the hospital. That was nice of you. But it didn't work. When you said, "Our group just sat in the field at recess and made those little bird nests out of ripped-up grass," it made me remember the dusty, almost-summer smell of grass in the field, the feel of the hot sun on my head, the semiprivate feeling of sitting in a circle and having a little piece of the field to ourselves, even though a couple of hundred kids are screaming and running all around us. It made me ache with remembering. It made me miss you guys—you and Katie and Jess and Sarah and Viv. It made me miss everything.

I'll still be a part of the group when I get out of here, won't I, Nina? It's silly, but you start realizing when you're away that things actually go on without you. Which of course they would, and you know this in your brain, but secretly you hope that maybe everyone constantly talks about how much they miss you and wishes you were there all the time. Stupid, I know. Maybe you think that way to avoid thinking about the possibility that you'll be forgotten.

Hey, we'll go make bird nests when I get out, right, Nina? We'll sit in the school field with the sun and the grass and do nothing but pluck up the grass and make it into bird nests. Maybe with little stone eggs?

You know when you get sick and miss a day of school? Kind of fun, right? But then, if you're sick for more than a few days, it gets less fun. You get bored. And then you start imagining that everyone at school, everyone in the world really, is having the best time of their *lives*. You think they're all having a huge party, even though they're probably just doing the usual school and work stuff. But somehow the usual things—going to class, running at recess, soccer practice—become more special because you can't be a part of them. It's a sad and lonely feeling, like being outside in the cold and looking through a window into a cozy, warm house.

That's the feeling I have here. It feels like everyone in the world is at a party except for me. Only here the party is *outside*, and I'm *inside* looking out. I watch the hospital workers heaving those bags of hospital filth into the dumpsters, and I actually envy them. What fun that would be, slinging waste into a dumpster, breathing fresh air, feeling the sun warm your face...I'm sounding pathetic, and I didn't mean to.

I know it's been a few days since I've written. I decided to have pity on you. You can only read so many freaked-out, depressing letters from a friend written at 0200 hours. And honestly, how often can you read about me taking little dancing Missy Wong for a slow walk up and down the halls?

My new policy is to write only when there is some actual news.

And there is some today! Brace yourself— it's ghastly. Is there any other kind of news in a hospital?

When I woke up this morning, I got out of bed and started to push Ivy to the washroom. But when I looked down, I noticed that my hand that was pushing her (the hand with the needle in it) looked nothing like a *hand* anymore! It was swollen so much that it looked like a pillow with a fringe of fingers. Or like a balloon. Or like a hand kids draw when they're two years old—just a big circle with five short stick fingers. To tell you the truth, it looked more like a *foot*. A fat baby's foot.

I gasped and looked up at Ivy. She swung her bag head apologetically. I skittered her over to the nurse call button and laid on that thing for dear life. When nobody came immediately, I panicked, and I pushed Ivy over to the door. I actually lifted her, because her wheels were sticking and this was an emergency.

We were just in time to collide with the Fussbudget.

Have I told you about her, Nina? Okay, quick summary here, and then we'll get back to the emergency. The Fussbudget is one of the nurses. A worrier. A ditherer. She's always dropping things, papers flutter out of the charts she carries, she takes ages to do things other nurses do in seconds, and her frizzy hair is always in her eyes. Worse, she talks about how bad she is at things, which, from a patient's perspective, is really terrible. You can be bad at your job. Fine. But telling everybody about it—specifically, people who are affected by it—is way, way worse.

So the Fussbudget is exactly, precisely, *not* the nurse you want in a crisis, definitely not the nurse you want around when your hand looks like it's going to blow up any second.

"The hand, the *hand*," I panted, pointing at my hand. I already seemed to be refusing ownership of it. Could that giant, mutant thing actually be mine?

"Holy *cow*!" she cried, her mouth dropping open. "That thing is *huge*!"

You see what I mean, Nina? She's hopeless.

The Fussbudget looked around wildly, as if she was hoping somebody competent would arrive to help both of us out. I half thought of running back to the call button to get somebody else. But the Fussbudget dumped the stuff she was carrying on a chair (where some of it slid to the germy floor) and said, "You should...back...bed!" She made vague shooing motions with her arms.

"What's wrong?" I wailed, scuttling back into bed. "Is it my bones? Am I going to die??" Not proud of that part, Nina, but if you saw that hand, you'd understand.

"No, no, no." The Fussbudget pushed her hair out of her face and prodded the hand with one tentative finger, like it was an experiment. Like she was testing to see if a cake in the oven was done. Her finger left little white circle indents on the puffy, reddish surface of my hand. It did not seem a very medical or scientific test.

"Needle's slipped...must've happened..."

That's how the Fussbudget talks. She starts a sentence, then trails off. This is usually just annoying. But when you fear for your life and the safety of your actual *hand*, it is infuriating. White-hot rage galloped through me.

"What? Ivy's slipped *how*? It must've happened *when*?" I snapped.

"Have to pull...redo the thingy...be right back..." The Fussbudget trotted away, murmuring to herself. I sat, glaring straight in front of me. I glanced up at Ivy. She seemed tense too. Finally, the Fussbudget clattered back, pushing a little trolley. She spilled cotton balls onto the bed as she set up shop. A roll of tape fell off the bed and wheeled in a curving arc under one of the other beds.

"So this will someday look like a *hand* again?" I asked, trying to keep my voice level. "Right? Just a normal hand?"

She fumbled with her supplies, pawing through them uncertainly.

"Oh, yes. Where is...oh, there. Hmm? Um-hum. A hand..." She reached for Ivy.

Honestly, Nina, I could have screamed. In fact, I was very, very close to screaming. You know when you make that kind of high-pitched *mmm, mmmm* sound deep in your throat, which is the sound of a scream being stifled? Maybe you don't know it. I do. I was making that sound. I was also shaking.

Finally, when I wouldn't hold out my hand, the Fussbudget glanced up at my face. She seemed surprised there was a person attached to the hand.

"Will…my…hand…go…back…to…normal?" I spoke slowly and quietly through clenched teeth.

The Fussbudget looked at me blankly. "Of course. Don't worry about *that*! Now where is…"

After ripping off the tape holding the useless needle in, she yanked it out. I will spare you her four excruciating, fumbling attempts to shove Ivy's needle back into a vein, any vein. She kept sighing, pushing back her hair and muttering confidence-inspiring things like "Shoot!" and "Nope, missed it again!" and "Why can't I *do* this?" I gasped, flinched and clenched with each jab, especially the one where she winced and said, "Ooh, sorry, *that* one must've hurt!" Yes, yes, it did, as a matter of fact. My arm was a searing lump of pain. I actually felt sick with pain.

Finally, mercifully, on the fifth attempt she muttered, "Oh, I give up!" and started packing up her instruments of torture. On the one hand, I was relieved, because there didn't seem to be any way she could get that needle in. All of my veins were literally shrinking away from her. But on the other hand, I was worried. The needle in my hand was my link to the medicine I need so my leg gets better and doesn't have to be *amputated*. I rubbed my pillow-hand and couldn't even enjoy the momentary sensation of freedom from Ivy before I panicked about what on earth we were going to do.

In the end, the Fussbudget called in a specialized, professional needle putter-inner (hospitals have those magical people, apparently) who in a matter of *seconds* calmly and painlessly slipped that needle right in, just a little farther up. Honestly, Nina, I barely felt it!

"Could you put a *ton* of tape on it? Like, wrap that sucker up good and solid? Just use as much tape as you need—more, even—so that it doesn't slip out again," I pleaded, chatting too much, not wanting the needle lady to leave, wanting her, in fact, to camp out in one of the visiting chairs in case the needle slipped out again.

"There," she said, after taping me up like a linebacker in a football game. "Solid. It's not going anywhere. And your hand will just absorb the extra liquid. Swelling'll probably be gone by tomorrow." She patted my shoulder and left.

So casual. So simple. So easy.

I'd like to say the Fussbudget was watching and taking notes, but she wasn't. She was fussing around, dropping things out of her pocket while gathering up the mess of bloody cotton balls and wads of tape that littered the bed and floor.

I didn't even care. My hand, and my bones, are feeling all of them just FINE.

Your calmer and much-less-puffy friend,
Kasey

Fourteen

Dear Nina,

Louise and the snack trolley came around again this evening. I asked Louise about the schedule—she comes Tuesdays, Thursdays and sometimes Friday or Saturday. I tried to be casual and cool about it, but I wasn't fooling her. She probably knows I *live* for these snacks, that this trolley is, sadly and pathetically, the highlight of my whole, entire life. She seems to understand.

"Saved you a couple bags of pretzels," Louise said, rummaging in the cart. "Got some decent-looking sandwiches too." Louise held up a triangular package and squinted at it. "Mystery meat."

"So bring me news of the outside world," I said to her like I always do and usually with my mouth full.

Louise has a nice, unexpected smile. "Don't worry. You're not missing anything. The outside world *sucks*, kid," she said.

"So does the inside hospital world," I said.

Louise gnawed on a hangnail. "You'll be out in a few weeks. Into the *outside*, sucky world. But without a gimpy leg. Well, not *without* it. Hey, leave one of those applesauces for Missy Wong—she likes those. And a pudding for Sadie. She's got, like, three teeth."

These are the kinds of conversations we have, Nina. But I love it when Louise comes around and sits and talks. Most people who come talk while they're doing things—changing Ivy's fluids, sweeping the floor, bringing a tray. Even visitors like my parents and grandparents don't just sit and talk about anything. They want to talk about me and my leg. And I want to talk about anything else.

Louise speaks like she's in a hurry. She blurts. She told me she used to stutter, which must have been awful as a kid. Imagine the frustration of knowing what you're going to say but not being able to get your mouth to cooperate in saying it. As a champion talker myself, I would *hate* that.

When we talk, I find out interesting things about high school, and about Louise's life. She loves animals and volunteers at a dog-rescue place, she wants to paint her room a very, very dark, almost-black blue, she writes "garbage" poetry and likes a smart guy named Devon. She'll say things like "he's so lame," but I know she likes him. She and her mom fight all the time, and she says it's a relief to come to her hospital job sometimes, even though the pay isn't great, just to stay out of the house. She doesn't talk about her dad.

We also talk about the hospital and the people who work here, which I find interesting. For example, I did not know that Rosie has a little daughter with a disability. I didn't know that one of the night nurses has a son who goes to high school with Louise and is, in her words, "not a bad guy but a total druggie." I always thought total druggies *were* bad guys. And the Bouncer once reported Louise for her attitude, which she admits is not good at all around the Bouncer.

"How is Missy Wong?" I asked. I hadn't seen her for a few days.

"Sick," Louise said. "They got her drugged up so she can't wander around. Caught her the other night trying to go upstairs." She gnawed on her thumbnail. "These old folks. Sure, they're taken care of. But some of them have no family. Nobody visits them. Like, ever. Which, when you think about it, *really* sucks."

We sat thinking about this.

"*You* visit them," I pointed out.

"Yeah. I try to talk a bit with each of them. Hey, you should help me. Want to?"

I jumped at that offer, Nina! I told Louise we could pretend to be relatives going to visit our great-grandparents. She could be my big sister (I always wanted a big sister), and I could be her little one. I do talk a lot, don't I?

Louise gave me a funny look. I think she would have liked to have a sister too. She didn't say that, but I got that feeling.

Louise let me push the snack cart down the hall while she pushed Ivy. I felt kind of important, having a semiofficial role. Being visitors as well, we sat and talked with anyone who was awake and seemed lonely.

Sometimes the conversations weren't what I was expecting. One of the old guys who used to be a farmer wanted to know how high the wheat was this year. The *wheat*, Nina. Louise said that was a good question and she'd make a point of finding out for him. One woman with watery blue eyes told us in detail about her wedding, which was probably sixty years ago but sounded very fancy. Another woman spoke a bit of Arabic for us, because she used to live in Egypt.

Of course, some of the old people whose memories weren't so good thought we actually *were* their relatives, some mistook us for nurses, some were just happy to chat a little about things in their room— some flowers by their bed, a photo, the food on the cart. Some of them didn't want us to leave.

I knew how they felt. I wished Louise worked there every day.

Maybe I'll get to go around with the cart again on Thursday, if my big sister doesn't mind.

Your friend who is getting way better at talking with old people,
Kasey

Fifteen

Dear Nina,

Last night I was woken up in the worst way ever possible in the history of waking up. And trust me, I've woken to Molly screaming, and Lizzy muttering in her deep, scary sleep voice, and Squeakers jumping on my back, and once Kyle *threw up in my ear.* That was years ago, but I don't believe I ever told you about that one. Mom was holding him and leaning over me to get to Molly in the dark. You know what? Let's just leave it there. I think I've said enough.

Anyway, Nina, don't go thinking, There goes Kasey, being all dramatic again. I'm really not.

This horrible thing that happened in the night makes my bloated hand seem like a funny little joke.

Here's how it went.

So I was lying in my bed, actually asleep—which is quite an achievement for me here. Usually I'm wandering around, reading or writing to you in the dark, creepy zerosomethingsomething hours.

CRASH! A violent, smashing sound snapped me instantly, heart-attackingly awake. It was like a whole cart of glass had been pushed over. There was thudding, and the sound of voices. Something terrible and violent was going on in the hall just outside my door. A man's voice was yelling and swearing. Swearing like you wouldn't believe, Nina. Not just one or two swears. A whole *list* of them.

Scuffling, banging noises, other voices, something smacked against the wall…

At this point I was sitting straight up in my bed, so wide awake I couldn't imagine ever sleeping again. I had goose bumps everywhere I can goose-bump, one hand was locked around Ivy's pole body, and the other had pulled the covers up to my eyes. I considered hiding in the closet or running into the bathroom, but I remembered what a struggle it is to get Ivy in there, and I didn't want to be caught out in the open when there was some kind of midnight brawl happening. So I lay there staring at the open door (because of course it's open) of my room, my heart thumping and my imagination going wild. Was there an escaped convict out there? A criminal? A *murderer*? I'm not proud of it, Nina, but *red-eyed clown puppet attack* also flitted through my brain. That stupid movie has a lot to answer for.

The muffled thudding and shouting continued, as if people (or puppets) were in some desperate wrestling match out there. I was *whimpering*, I was that scared.

Crack! My door was thrown open by a huge man in a hospital gown. His robe was swinging open, and his hospital gown was wrenched off one shoulder. His face was red and sweaty, his grizzled gray hair was standing on end, and he was roaring, "HERE, KITTY, KITTY, KITTY!" He stomped wildly, frantically around the room, his cowboy boots making a heck of a racket on the hospital floors.

I swear I'm not making this up. Also, it was definitely not a dream. It's actually very annoying when people say, "Oh, that must have been a dream!" when it wasn't. Not that you'd say that, Nina. I meant other people.

Anyway, I sank under my blankets as the man swung over to the closet by my bed and flung both doors open. Thank goodness I didn't hide in there!

"KITTY! *KITTY*!"

Two nurses surged into the room seconds later (which felt like hours), followed by a couple of porters. They tried to grab the man's arms, but he shrugged them off like they were flies and stomped into the middle of the room. He turned to my bed, and even though he looked straight at me, he looked *through* me, if you know what I mean. Like, if his brain could talk, it would just be noting "beds, things, table, NOT KITTY," rather than "terrified girl."

One of the night nurses, the one who competes in triathlons and who is my new superhero, ran between me and the scary man. She raised her voice. "KEN! KEN! MR. BOYCHUK! You're scaring Kasey! You're scaring this little girl."

The other night nurse said soothingly, "Let's get you back to your own room, buddy."

He didn't seem to hear them, just kept looking around frantically, calling for his kitty, kitty, kitty.

Sometimes my brain blanks out in a crisis, Nina, but sometimes it goes into hyper idea mode. I was thinking, Run, hide, be quiet, stay still, all those things. But then I thought, It's all about some cat. Find this man a kitty! No real kitties around, obviously, but maybe a fake one would help. I reached under my blankets for the pile of stuffies that Molly had hauled in for me in that germy green garbage bag.

As Ken and the nurses yelled back and forth, not really at each other but just generally, I found what I was looking for. It was a mangy cat stuffie I've had for years. You know how you have things for years, Nina, and sometimes you look at them and wonder why? We've talked about this before because of that orange stuffie you have that neither of us knows what it *is*.

Anyway, I'd named this stuffed cat Whiskers when I was probably, like, three, and it had always sat with all my other stuffies on my shelf (or in the hospital, under the covers, near the foot of the bed.) Its black fur is matted. It has a little miserable, frowning face, which probably is what prevented it from becoming one of my A-list stuffies. Strangely, it has no whiskers, which makes you wonder about the name.

"Okay, Whiskers, hope this is okay with you," I whispered.

I leaned over and shoved Whiskers into the nurse's hand just while she was in mid-yell. "…and we'll *find* your kitty—what the—oh, hey, *HERE* SHE IS, KEN! FOUND HER! *HERE'S* YOUR KITTY!"

The huge old man stopped and swung around from wrestling with one of the porters.

His desperate face crumpled. He stumbled over and took Whiskers in his arms like she was a precious baby. He gently stroked her dull, matted fake fur with a huge, shaky, bony hand, leaning over her protectively, as though he was worried someone would snatch her away.

I saw his face, Nina, and I wish I hadn't. He looked confused and upset and happy and dazed and terrified all at once, tears snaking down his craggy, flushed cheeks. I looked away. Poor old Ken. It's not fair to look at someone when their poker face isn't working anymore, when every confused thing in their brain is out there for the whole world to see.

"There you go, Ken. There, see? Got your cat now." Triathlon-Hero rubbed the big man's shoulder and talked quietly and kindly to him while the other nurse jabbed at the intercom, telling somebody to "contact the night resident about sedation. Stat."

They persuaded Ken back to his room at 0243 hours (2:43 AM). He was still clutching the cat, and he seemed completely different—shrunken, hunched and old, old, old. His cowboy boots even seemed too big for him.

Triathlon-Hero (whose name is Jackie, actually) came back in a few minutes to see if I was okay. Even though I did the "oh, I'm fine" thing (because I'm a big girl and a brave girl, as everyone keeps telling me), she sat down on my bed beside me like she didn't really believe me. And I was glad she didn't.

"Sorry about that, Kasey. That must have been scary for you. That was the worst Ken's been in the two years I've been here. He's usually such a sweetie, a real gentleman. He has dementia, a disease old people sometimes get where they really don't know what they're doing. Or they don't know their own families or friends. Their minds don't work properly. It sometimes makes them upset and hard to reason with." We sat together, both of us thinking what a sad, hard life that would be, to be a stranger in your own life.

"I feel sorry for him," I said.

"I know, honey. So do I. But," the nurse said brightly, "he's happy right now. And right now is what matters for most of these old folks. Not the past or the future, but *right now*. You're a total hero for the quick thinking about the cat." She gave my shoulder a little punch. "Kasey saves the day! Well, actually, the night. We'll get your cat back, but maybe Ken could borrow her for a little while?"

"He can keep her," I said quickly. "Don't take her away from him. Please don't. He needs her more than I do."

I won't ever see Whiskers again, but I don't mind. Maybe we all have a purpose, Nina, even grumpy, mangy, semiforgotten stuffies. Maybe her purpose is to comfort a confused and desperate old man who can't figure things out for himself anymore.

And that's not actually such a sad story, is it?

Your friend who is so tired her eyes are crossing,
Kasey

Sixteen

Dear Nina,

I have officially become a night creature. Nocturnal, like those scuttling, furtive animals in the dark room at the zoo. I wonder if my eyes are getting bigger and rounder. (Next time you visit, tell me if you think they are. It's hard to tell when you see yourself every day.) Between the death-snorer, the red-eyed clown puppets, and poor old Ken, I haven't had great luck in the sleep department. Honestly, can you really blame me for being afraid to go to sleep?

Somehow, lying in bed waiting for something to happen makes things worse. It makes me feel like a target. So I wander. Ivy and I have perfected the art of gliding soundlessly through the hallways, her on her smooth, wheely feet, me in my slippers, the bottoms of which must be so incredibly germy that I don't even want to think about it. *Teeming* with billions and billions of germs. There's no way I'm bringing them home or even into our van. I am throwing them in the hospital garbage the second I can leave here.

There are only two nurses on at night, and the really sick (and sad) patients in rooms 216 and 217 keep them pretty busy. I've heard the nurses talk about the people in those rooms, and they all seem to have a ton of medical problems as well as being old. The nurses, amazingly, seem to be able to stay cheerful even though it must be a hard job to nurse very sick old people. I can't even imagine how sad and depressing that could be. But they're still *people*, after all, right? They were once even kids like us! Maybe they even still feel young on the inside.

Anyway, night in the hospital is a secret time, a quiet time. Down at the end of the hall, in my room, it's a scary time. But when I get out of my room, it helps me remember that it's still the hospital, still the same people. Nothing changes just because it's nighttime. Or so I tell myself.

Oh, who am I kidding, Nina? Have you ever wandered around your house, or even your room, in the dark? It feels different. Not *necessarily* spookier or creepier, but with the definite *possibility* of it feeling spookier and creepier. I think it's the actual darkness that's the problem. Darkness with only a hint of light creates shadows that make things look weirder, which makes a person jumpier and creeped outier. Goose bumpier. It makes things look different, sometimes only slightly different, like in a dream where your mom looks mostly like your mom, but then she does something and you think in your dream brain, That's not really Mom at all.

The night is when you make discoveries. I've discovered that the two night nurses are friends. I've told you about Jackie, the hero-triathlete who was so nice to Ken. I call the other nurse the Night Owl, which isn't even very clever, because if you asked anybody what animal she most resembles, they would say "owl" before you'd even finished the question. She's plump, with feathery hair, a little hook nose and big round glasses. And she wears fluffy sweaters draped over her shoulders that billow out when she walks. I'm always relieved she doesn't have a mouse in her beak.

The Night Owl says her son (the one that goes to school with Louise) has "got in with a bad crowd," and both of the nurses don't like one of the doctors at all. I believe I heard the words "arrogant jerk." I've also discovered that the Bouncer, though she bounces by day, isn't very popular with the night staff either. They seem to think she deliberately hides things to make it seem like the unit can't operate without her.

I know, I know, this sounds boring or worse—like I'm a complete creeper eavesdropper. But actually, when you live here like I do, it's interesting. A hospital unit is like a very small town, and you know me—I like to know what's going on.

I discovered something last night. Or should I say some*one*? At 0310 hours (3:10 AM), I turned the corner in the hall, and there in front of me, alone and unprotected, was Missy Wong! She was *out of her wheelchair*, walking! Actually, kind of shuffling very slowly down the hall away from her room, heading for the doors to the unit! She looked very tiny, like a little girl in the K-4 hallway at school. Her thin white hair was brushed back from her face, released from those ridiculous pigtails, and her shawl had slipped from one shoulder, the long black fringe trailing along the germy floor. In all the times I've sat with her and pushed her down the hall, I've never seen her upright without her wheelchair, let alone without her pigtails. It made me feel strange, Nina, like when you see your mom or dad asleep, or when our teacher takes off her glasses and rubs her moist, pink eyes and doesn't really look like Mrs. D. at all until she puts them back on.

Missy Wong was leaning with both hands on the long railing running the length of the hall, and her pink slippers moved more up and down than forward, if you know what I mean. Up and down, up and down. Her little feet moved like they remembered they had to move in order for walking to happen, but they'd forgotten exactly how walking actually worked. They moved like puppet feet on strings. I wondered how long it had taken her to get that far.

"Missy Wong!" I whispered, wheeling Ivy down the hall toward her. No answer. She didn't pause or even turn her head.

"Missy Wong!" I tried again, walking right up beside her and putting a hand on her shoulder. She gave a sort of startled jump, and I jumped at her jump, and Ivy skittered and clattered, and we all did a group flail until I steadied her.

"It's okay, it's okay. Just me." I giggled nervously and pointed at myself, smiling and nodding. "Just Kasey. You must be cold." I picked up her shawl and wrapped it around her. I looked around for a nurse, but the hallway was deserted.

Missy Wong looked different. Excited. Lit up. She smiled her toothless grin, tilted her nodding head, grabbed my hand and pulled me with her toward the door, as if she'd been waiting for me. If she could have spoken, she might have said,

"Oh, good, you're here. Hurry, let's go!" Her feet stamped up and down in a restless, impatient way.

"I'm not sure we can...I don't think we're allowed...we should go back," I stammered, sounding annoying and exactly like the Fussbudget. Missy Wong paused, took my hand in both of hers and jabbed it down at her shawl, then up at the ceiling. She gave me the feeling that this was urgent, important.

"You want to go upstairs?" I asked. She looked down at the shawl, smoothing her tiny, wrinkled hand over the colorful embroidery, over the peacock and the stars and the river. And her feet started up with that dancing up-and-down motion.

The Night Owl rounded the corner up ahead and stopped when she saw us.

"And just what are you two doing out of bed? It's the middle of the night!" She hurried toward us, her open sweater wings flapping.

I explained that Missy Wong seemed to want to go upstairs, but the Night Owl shook her head, took charge of her and steered the old woman around in a brisk U-turn.

"She doesn't know what she wants, Kasey," she said. "She's never even been upstairs. What on earth would she want with Urology? Or the cardiac unit? That's all that's upstairs. She's just confused. AREN'T WE, MISSY WONG? ARE WE A LITTLE CONFUSED? WE NEED TO GET BACK TO BED, DON'T WE?"

The Night Owl looked over at me. "Are you okay, Kasey? Do you want me to stop by your room after I settle Missy Wong? Do you need anything?"

"No, I'm fine. Just couldn't sleep." It was nice of her to ask, but I said what she expected me to say. I'm a big girl, a brave girl, remember. When you're big and brave, how can you say, "Yes, please come by and talk to me about your teenager getting in with a bad crowd and being not a bad guy even though he's a total druggie, and about the doctor who's a jerk, and how it feels being a human owl and really anything you want to talk about to help me get through another long, scary night." How can you say things like that? You can't.

But I wasn't fine. Because when I looked at Missy Wong, when I said goodnight, I saw that all the light had drained out of her face. She wasn't dancing anymore or even nodding. She hung her head and looked terribly old and very tired. I couldn't shake the feeling that somehow I'd failed her, that somehow I hadn't understood.

What do you think? If you have any advice, Nina, I'd be glad to hear it.

Your friend, the hospital hall roamer,
Kasey

Seventeen

Dear Nina,

Are you sitting down? *Huge* news! But first, you might want to put on gloves to read this letter—in fact, I strongly advise you to. And after you finish it, wash your hands with soap and warmish to hot water for as long as it takes you to sing "Happy Birthday" *twice*. Promise? The reasons for these complicated instructions will become clear.

I am now allowed to be even more paranoid than usual about germs, Nina. Legitimately paranoid.

Our unit is under quarantine! Isolated! Separated from the rest of the hospital! Roped off!

We have a terrible, germy, very contagious illness oozing invisibly through the rooms and possibly infecting all the patients! So we've been sealed off from the rest of humanity so we don't spread the disease to anyone but ourselves. But help! I'm thinking of the "ourselves" part of that sentence, the people in this unit. Are we all going to be sacrificed so this disease doesn't spread to the rest of the world? I've never felt more like escaping.

Everyone is panicking quietly. Me—not so quietly. This is an example of how I greet people coming into my room:

Random nurse or aide: Hi, Ka—

Me (interrupting): SANITIZE YOUR HANDS! WHERE'S YOUR MASK? KEEP YOUR DISTANCE! DON'T TOUCH ME! DON'T TOUCH *ANYTHING*! DON'T BREATHE ON ME!

I'm not even exaggerating, Nina. All the staff have to wear these paper robes and masks and gloves whenever they go into a patient's room, and then throw them away when they leave. That's how bad it is! We're using *disposable clothes*, the germs are so dangerous. Even visitors have to wear them!

The place looks like a sinister science-fiction movie. Mom and Dad have stopped bringing my brothers and sisters, so they don't get sick. Now Mom's stopped coming because she's nursing the baby, and nobody wants him to get sick. And Mom's freaking out, worrying that I'll get sick, and her freaking out is making me freak out, so we're freaking out in jittery circles. I told her to stay home and stay healthy.

So Dad has been my only visitor for the last few days. I make him wear gloves and a mask, because, of course, he doesn't think about these things very deeply. He's all "Hey, Pumpkin, how's it going?" in this cheerful voice, as if I'm not drowning in deadly bacteria and teetering on the brink of a desperate and terrible illness! Not good, Dad, not good. Honestly, Nina, I love him, you know I love him, but I want to shake him sometimes.

I read the notices about this disease—every single one of them. Even the private nurses-only ones in the nurses' lounge area. And now, having quite enough information about this disease, I have officially barricaded myself in my room.

The disease is called *C. difficile*, which is such a stupid name for a disease. There shouldn't be an abbreviation for something in a serious disease, am I right? *C.* What does *that* stand for? And why aren't they telling us? It makes it seem like there's something somebody's hiding. But besides that, *C. difficile* sounds creepy and oddly *French* somehow. I think it must be French, because of the way you pronounce it. Like it rhymes with bloodthirsty *eel*.

What annoys me is that diseases should end in *itis*, as everyone knows (tonsill*itis*, appendi-*citis*, even my osteo-something-something-*itis*). And if they don't, their names should clearly describe the actual disease rather than leaving a person guessing. That's only fair.

I can't get a straight answer about what the mysterious *C.* stands for. The nurses' notice said something like *Clostrilium* (which sounds like a plant with possibly purple flowers—to me anyway). The Fussbudget said something about "colon," made a wrinkly nosed you-don't-want-to-know face and shook her head vaguely. Very helpful.

It's definitely something to do with evil and cunning bacteria (there was also something in there about "spores"—what the heck is a spore?) multiplying into more and more toxic bacteria and making everyone so sick they have to go to the bathroom almost constantly. I know that's a fairly disgusting, nontechnical explanation, but that pretty much sums it up.

And that's not all. The notices also said that this disease can be very serious, leading even to *death*! I swear they say that, Nina. In fact, I'd pull one off the wall and send it to you as proof, but I don't want to C. *difficile*-bomb you and your whole house. Those bacteria are real survivors, apparently, and can last for months on things, and how do you scrub paper? You'll have to take my word for it.

C. difficile, my notices tell me, is especially dangerous to old people and children! Well, hmm…let's see. Who do we have on this unit? I know! Old people and a child! And yet, Nina, nobody seems to be panicking quite enough for my liking. I'd like to have sirens wailing, lights flashing, gowned and masked people running around *doing something,* and the strong, strong reek of detergent and sanitizer in the halls. Also, those fire-blaster guns they use in action movies would come in very handy. Or can *C. difficile* bacteria even survive *fire*? Calm, Kasey, calm.

I'm very worried for my old people here. So I'm taking precautions. I'm washing my hands probably fifty times a day and trying not to touch anything, including Ivy (she understands). I wear surgical gloves when I'm not washing my hands. I wear a mask as well, which gets hot from just my breathing and makes my voice sound like Darth Vader's ("*hrhhh, hrhh, hrhhhh*"). I am also helpfully reminding all the staff about gowning and gloving and masking whenever I see them. Rosie calls me the "unit cop."

So don't come to visit, Nina, until I give you the *all clear.*

Stay away. Stay healthy. Scrub your hands.

Your friend in the fight against this deadly disease,
Kasey
PS. Burn this letter.

Eighteen

Dear Nina,

We have been under this plague for six days now.

Unfortunately, some of the old folks have gotten very sick. Missy Wong has—I haven't seen her for days. I hope she's okay. She's so old and so little. I made her a card and have been drawing her pictures to cheer her up. They aren't very good. It's hard to draw well when you're wearing rubber gloves, I've discovered. Especially adult-sized rubber gloves. Anyway, I sure hope she gets better soon. It's funny how you can miss somebody who doesn't actually even speak!

I miss you too, Nina. I've missed writing to you, because when I write to you I have a very clear picture of you in my head. And after I finish a letter, I feel like we've talked, even though it's just me moaning about being in the hospital. I deliberately haven't written to you, to avoid germing up your house. You're not sick, are you? I haven't got a letter from you for a while, so I hope you're not sick.

I have to tell you something. It's a total secret though. Don't tell anybody, especially my Mom. Here's what happened.

I was lying in bed today. Do I even have to say that, I wonder? Lying in bed seems to be all I do. There was nothing on the two channels of television (you can only watch preschool cartoons and boring golf so much), and I've read and reread all the books I have (Dad should be bringing in a new batch soon). So there I was, lying and staring at the clock, watching that smooth, red second hand swoop around and around. I'd peeked out of my doorway a little bit earlier to see how the infectious-disease stuff was going. There were a few rattling carts and gowned figures gliding around over by the desk. But it was pretty lonely at my end of the hall. So I shut the door, crawled back into bed and watched the clock.

There was a knock on the door. This was odd. As I've told you before, almost nobody knocks in a hospital. And it was too early for "dinner" (which, by the way, has not improved).

"Who is it?" I called warily, slipping on my mask and grabbing the pumper of hand sanitizer that Rosie gave me.

Lizzy's head poked around the door. Yes, Nina, *that* Lizzy. *My* Lizzy. My little sister! She slipped in, closed the door after her and pushed her mask up onto the top of her head.

"Hi, Kasey," she said, as if there was nothing unusual about her wandering into the hospital in the middle of a life-threatening epidemic. Well, hopefully at the *end* of a life-threatening epidemic.

"Lizzy!" I struggled to sit up in bed. Ivy swayed her bag head and looked over in watery interest at my eight-year-old sister. "What are you doing here? Where are Mom and Dad?"

"Oh, Mom's at home with the others," Lizzy said. "Dad's down the hall at the desk, asking the nurses a bunch of questions. He's being," she said conspiratorially, "a *distraction*." She came over and sat on the side of the bed. She was wearing a baggy hoodie and walked with her arms around her middle, like she was hugging herself. "I just thought I haven't seen you for a while," she said calmly. "And I promised you…" She unzipped the hoodie and out popped our little dog!

"Squeakers!" I cried, as she jumped all over the bed, frantically wagging her whole back end like she does when she's really, really excited. She covered my face with little dog-lick kisses. I was so happy to see her! Nobody can convince you you've been missed quite like a dog can.

I told Lizzy she shouldn't have come. I told her that she could get sick, Dad should have known better, that the hospital people wouldn't like a dog being brought into the hospital, that she should have a gown, and gloves…

"But it's just for, like, five minutes," Lizzy said. "You haven't seen Squeakers for so long! So I told

Dad I needed him to drive me and Squeakers to the hospital for *five minutes*. We came up the back stairs, and we didn't touch anything or see anybody. And I've only got five minutes and then I have to meet Dad back downstairs! It's exciting! Our secret, Kasey—between you and me and Dad. And Squeakers."

"Our secret!" I laughed. After weeks of nothing but hospital rules, I'd forgotten that some people don't live by them. I cuddled my dog's wiggly little body, wishing she and Lizzy could both stay. "You should go though. What if somebody sees you leave?"

"Well, I thought of that," Lizzy said slowly. "They pretty much would have to forgive me. I mean, they couldn't put me in jail or anything."

She was right. I have to remember how Lizzy thinks. It's a different way of thinking than anyone else I know. It *is* sometimes easier to ask forgiveness than get permission.

"You're a wonderful sister, Lizzy," I said, stroking Squeakers' silky ears and feeling like I was going to cry. "Thank you so much for coming."

I gave her a hug. "But you should go now. Wash your hands *hard* when you get home, *for a long time*. Lots of soap. In fact, have a bath too. Okay? Promise?"

"Promise."

She gave me a hard, awkward hug.

We stuffed Squeakers back down the hoodie ("It's just until we get outside, Squeakers," I heard Lizzy murmur), and she opened the door, looked out, turned and gave me a thumbs-up and a little wave, and then Lizzy was gone.

It was the happiest five minutes of my whole hospital life.

Your friend who's letting you in on the secret,
Kasey

Nineteen

Dear Nina,

I'm in training.

Yes, I'm in the hospital, and true, I do not have the use of my left arm. I also come attached to my training partner, Ivy (who, by the way, never complains about our fitness program—she's a good sport). Also, the mask and gloves and gown are not optimal. But my bones are feeling all of them fine, just FINE, and I need to do *something* to stay well. I seemed to be lying in bed a lot, not even reading. Just staring at the clock or out the window and feeling depressed.

My grandma wrote me a letter (and sent a box of cookies, which I inhaled in about an hour). Anyway, in the letter she said that when she broke her leg, she did all kinds of exercises *right in her bed*. So that got me thinking, and now I have a plan.

I, Kasey Morgan, am determined to stay as healthy as humanly possible. How does a person do this? Obviously, by eating right and exercising. Everyone knows that. I can't do much about the food bit (don't get me started on the almost-cold beef-like substance and smeary peas in a whitish "gravy" from last night—I'm gagging as I write). But I *can* exercise.

And let's face it. I *will* get out of here one day (in fact, in ten days!), and I don't want to be last in everything in our soccer practices when I do. And I feel happier about things now that I have a bit of a plan. More in control, less at the mercy of hospital life, less like a hospital *patient*.

Want to hear my training schedule? It's kind of pathetic, but I had to be creative. Remember that I don't exactly have a track or gym equipment here.

1) After breakfast (0800 hours):
   - ten fast laps of the unit (totally gowned and masked and not touching anything)
   - fifty squats in my room with the door closed
   - twenty Ivy lifts (she's not as light as she looks)
   - hand sanitizing
2) After lunch (1230 hours):
   - jogging hard on the spot for three sets of five minutes
   - twenty laps of my room *with lunges*
   - twenty book lifts with my heaviest *Harry Potter*
   - hand sanitizing
3) After dinner (1730 hours):
   - ten laps of the unit (gowned, masked and not touching anything)
   - fifty wall push-ups (using that left arm really carefully to avoid it blowing up again)
   - 50 sit-ups (there's no way I'm lying on that germy floor, so I do them in bed, which is harder)
   - hand sanitizing

4) Middle of the night (0230 hours)—Ideally, all the exercise will tire me out, so these are optional, for if I'm awake:
  - five laps of the unit (gowned, masked, etc.) if a nurse doesn't shoo me back to bed
  - fifty toe touches
  - stretching
  - hand sanitizing

Not much variety, but I'll let you know how it goes. I hope soccer is going well. That was a big win last week. Tell me, was Shelby's goal a fluke? It was, wasn't it? Knew it. Left midfielder's always been my position (everybody knows that), so I hope she hasn't gotten attached. That sounds kind of mean, but Nina, I miss it all so much. The running. The kicking. The sun, the grass, the air...Sorry, sounding a little pathetic here, and I didn't mean to.

Your friend in health and fitness,
Kasey

Twenty

Dear Nina,

Believe it or not, I am sitting outside. The sun feels strange and wonderful on my pale hospital skin. Don't worry, I haven't escaped.

You know that little patch of grass outside the hospital, right by the parking lot? Well, maybe you don't because it's just a little patch of grass by the parking lot. Anyway, that's where I am. Me and six of the old folks, all lined up in wheelchairs, like a special people-parking section. I should tell you that I'm only sitting in a wheelchair because there's nowhere else to sit. Ivy and I pushed my chair outside.

I'm beside Missy Wong, who keeps squinting up at the sky and plucking at her shawl. She's looking very thin and old and *sad* somehow, which just breaks my heart. She was sick with C. *difficile*, which has finally, thankfully, *mercifully* oozed out of our unit. Or so they told us anyway. I kept gowning and masking and handwashing for two more days to be extra sure. Where do those germy bacteria or viruses actually, technically go? I wonder. Do they die or sleep or what? Or does someone carry one or two of them on the bottom of their shoe (for example) to a whole other place where they multiply and spread and infect unsuspecting new people? Who knows? I hope Dad hasn't carried them home or to his work. If I were a germ, I'd definitely pick him to hop a ride on.

At first when we came outside (in a long, slow, wheely line of patients and nurses and porters), it seemed like a bit of a party, like those rare times we have class outside at school when the weather is nice. But now it's a bit of an ordeal, to be honest. Ken and the new guy (which makes him sound young, but he's not—*at all*) are asleep, two of the others are arguing loudly, and Sadie is asking *nonstop* what's for lunch. Believe me, Sadie, you don't want to know.

I feel like making a break for it across the parking lot. I could do it too, Nina—I could run right out of here! With all my training, I could definitely outrun the nurses and porters (the triathlon nurse isn't here). But there are curbs, so what would Ivy do? Plus, Rosie would be disappointed, and Louise wouldn't have anyone to help her with the snack cart, and Missy Wong wouldn't have anyone to push her down the hall, hold her hand, draw her pictures and cheer her up.

So here I sit, flexing my feet and itching to run but stopping myself.

Are you proud of me?

Your friend who challenges you to a race the second I get home,
Kasey

Twenty-One

Dear Nina,

Thank you so much for the stuffie! It's so cute and looks kind of like Squeakers, only with different colors. I'm calling her Sneakers, because she's got four black feet. She's officially a premium stuffie, a head-of-the-bed rather than a down-by-my-feet stuffie. I laughed at your card too. No, I'm not watching the evil-clown-puppet-movie sequel. Ever.

Boy, was it nice to get your present today, especially after Dr. Roberts's visit. Remember him? Dr. Robot? So he hasn't come by ONCE since this whole thing started, and he gave me the one-month sentence in this place. You'd think he might have checked in maybe once, right? Just to see that my leg hasn't actually fallen off? The lesser doctors (who are *way* nicer) have been by, but not the Robot himself.

So I was surprised when he and another doctor walked into my room this morning. I was doing my squats but stopped, obviously, when they came in. *Not* stopping doing the squats would have been hilarious, come to think of it. How weird would I have looked?

Anyway, here's how it went.

Dr. Robot (barely glancing at me while flipping through the chart): Well, ah, Katherine-Charlotte. How's the leg?

Me: Good. I've been doing—

Dr. Robot: Inflammation down. Good. Well, another month in the hospital should do it.

[DEAD SILENCE DURING WHICH I BELIEVE MY HEART ACTUALLY STOPPED]

Me: What??? WHAT???

Dr. Robot (barking laugh, like an alien that's taken over a human body and doesn't know how to do laughter yet): Mhar! Mhar!

Other Doctor: He's joking. Joking.

Dr. Robot: Did you see her face? You'd think she wasn't enjoying our hospitality! Mhar!

And here I thought Dr. Robot didn't have a sense of humor, Nina! Obviously he does. It's just a freakishly mean one! Mhar!

The nonalien other doctor paused at the door and gave me a two-thumbs-up sign and said, "End of next week you'll be outta here! Enjoy the rest of your summer!" Thank you, other doctor.

Your friend who is still shaking, and who officially hates Dr. Robot, but who only has a few days left,

Kasey

Twenty-Two

Dear Nina,

You remember how Lizzy broke all the rules by bringing Squeakers in here? Well, I broke some rules tonight—probably a lot of them—and I don't even care.

I was fast-walking my first lap of the unit, trying to tire myself out. It was about 2300 hours (11:00 PM). That's a very quiet time, by the way. The two night nurses have just taken over from the tired evening nurses, and most of the patients are asleep. The unit is pretty quiet, except for the death snorer and a patient who always calls out in her sleep.

I turned a corner and almost collided with—guess who? My old late-night, hall-walking buddy, Missy Wong! Alone, out of her wheelchair and making a break for it again. Only this time, she didn't look excited or happy. She looked desperate and determined. And, for her, she was moving pretty fast.

The Night Owl told me that Missy sometimes slips out of her bed at night even though they put up these rails and "secure her" so she won't fall out. It's for her own protection, the nurse said, because she could fall out of bed and break her hip or something. I'm glad she explained that to me, because if you don't know the reason for it, all these old people strapped and barricaded in their beds just looks mean.

Anyway, here she was, in the quiet back hallway, heading for the exit.

I pushed Ivy around in front of her and tried to talk to her, to look into her eyes. She didn't even pause, she was that focused. She has this way of looking at you as if she's not looking at you but at something bigger than you, if you know what I mean. As if you're only a piece of some big puzzle she's been doing for years inside her brain. She reminded me of my sister Lizzy, who thinks differently than pretty much anybody in the world. Maybe that's how I solved the problem—thinking like Lizzy.

Missy Wong grabbed my arm with her little bird hand and started hauling me along with her, like a little kid tugging at her mom. We lurched and leaned and shuffled forward until she stopped dead in the silence of that back hallway. She grabbed my hand with her shaky one and pointed it down at her shawl.

That shawl again. Always the shawl. Rosie told me that as long as she's worked here, she's never seen Missy Wong without it. They even have to wait until she's asleep to pull it away from her to wash it, and they get it back to her by the time she wakes up.

Was all this pointing at the shawl random? I wondered. Was it just that she was so old, and the shawl was so familiar, like one of my stuffies, that it was comforting to her to point at it and stroke it? Or was it more than that? Was there some meaning in the shawl, some message? What if she'd really been trying to say something, in Missy Wong shawl language, all this time? What if I tried her language for a change and really listened to her? It was like a mystery, Nina, and I felt like the shawl was the key.

She held out a part of the shawl with her free hand and ran my fingers over it with the other. I felt the thick, silky embroidery like it was a raised map. Over the tiny bumps of the people in the fields, around the swirls of the peacock's feathers, down the thick, smooth river. And, finally, up the winding, spiky dragon, up, up, up the tower to the stars. She stopped my fingers at the stars. And she held them there.

The *stars*! I remembered Louise saying she'd caught Missy Wong trying to get "upstairs." *I'd* found her trying to get upstairs before. Both times were at night. Maybe we'd just assumed she wanted to go upstairs because she was pointing up. Maybe *up* meant more than just upstairs. Maybe *up* meant up beyond the roof and into the sky and out into the universe. Maybe she wanted to *look* up at night and see the stars! Could it be that simple?

I circled my finger on the shawl's spiky, silvery stars. I thought about how Lizzy had brought in Squeakers against the rules. And about how rules made things easier for the people in charge but sometimes weren't so great for the people who had to live under them. I mean, some of these old people might actually want to eat dinner at, say, six o'clock. Or seven even. But dinner here, whether you like it or not, whether you're hungry or not, is at 5:00 PM (1700 hours). And as far as I can tell from my time here, they only get the old folks (and me) outside occasionally, and only during the day. Never at night.

When was the last time Missy Wong had seen the stars?

I thought about the nurses on duty tonight. The Night Owl and the Grumbler. Neither one of them would understand that Missy Wong wanted to go outside. The Night Owl knew her rules, and she'd cluck about patients needing to be in bed by 9:00 PM (2100 hours). She'd be cheerful about it, but there would be no way she'd say, "Sure, great idea! I'm a night creature myself, so I totally understand."

The Grumbler would see it as a stupid hassle involving more work. But I thought about how happy that five minutes with Squeakers had made me. Couldn't I give Missy Wong five minutes, just *five minutes*, with the stars?

"Missy Wong," I said, giving her arm a little pat, "let's go outside." I pointed up. Her feet started moving in that excited up-down way.

How does a kid smuggle a little old lady out of the hospital, Nina? Carefully. Quietly. And with a bit of luck. I remembered that the Grumbler was in room 216 because I'd just passed by there. I looked up at Ivy and her bag head nodded gently, agreeing with me. But where was the Night Owl?

You know how sometimes things work out even better than you'd hoped? That doesn't happen often, but every once in a while, it's a nice surprise. Like that time at school when I didn't even order the hot lunch (and instead had a smelly tuna sandwich on that dry, grainy bread Mom makes that I *hate*), but there was an extra pizza because William was sick so I got it? This was a bit like that. There was nobody at the unit desk. Nobody down the hall. Nobody near the elevators. And the elevator doors opened the second I pushed the Down button. It worked perfectly, even though my heart was hammering and I was bracing myself for a swoop from the Night Owl the whole time. Missy Wong just looked excited. The three of us got into the elevator without a problem. Ivy made a little noise rattling over the metal elevator bump, but she couldn't help it.

A quick ride down and we were on the main floor. We turned to the front doors, but there were people there, a security guard and a porter laughing about something.

"Think, Kasey, think." I started to sweat. "There must be another way." And then I remembered Lizzy saying she and Dad came up the back way. The *back* way. I looked down a hall behind us. There was a bright red Exit sign at the end.

I hustled Ivy and Missy Wong down the hallway. We were close now, so close.

I pushed open the door and we stood there, framed against the dark, smelling the fresh night air. Made it! Missy Wong started pushing past me to get outside. A voice floating out of the darkness made me jump.

"Should prop that door open, kid. It locks."

Louise! It was only Louise! Relief flooded through me. She was on the grass to the left of the door, sitting with her back against the building. She tossed a thick stick over. "I usually use that if I want to get back in."

"Thanks. What are you doing here, Louise?" She'd finished work hours earlier.

She stood up and dusted off her jeans. "Just didn't want to go home. Hey, Missy Wong." Her voice softened a little. "What are *you* doing all the way down here?"

"I think she wanted to see the *stars*, Louise. I think that's why she always wants to go upstairs. Not up*stairs*, but *up*. So I brought her outside.

Just for five minutes." I was talking while Louise helped Missy Wong sit down on her jean jacket. I lifted Ivy over because her wheels don't work so great on grass.

With the door mostly shut again, the darkness closed around us. It was quiet and still warm after the hot July day. The silky night air smelled of flowers and cut grass and *not* of hospital. I'd forgotten how wonderful the nonhospital world smells on a summer night. We sat in a row with our backs against the building. When you think about it, kind of a strange group—a sixteen-year-old, a ninety-four-year-old, a twelve-year-old and Ivy (I'm not sure what age she is).

"Well," said Louise, "you picked a gorgeous night."

I looked up. The blue-black sky was clear, and the stars were shining like they knew we needed them. I turned to Missy Wong eagerly to point up, to say, "See? Stars! Just the same as the stars on your shawl." But I didn't end up saying anything. I didn't need to.

In the faint light from the door, Missy Wong's round face was lifted to the stars. Her dark eyes glittered, and her mouth was open in a wide smile. Her tense little body had completely relaxed. She looked peaceful. She looked *young*. Like one of us kids.

"Good call, kid," said Louise out of the dark to my left. There was a smile in her voice.

I'll write more tomorrow, Nina, because there's more. It's zero hour—00:47 hours (12:47 AM). Early for me, but I'm so tired.

Your friend who plays by her own rules,
Kasey

Twenty-Three

Dear Nina,

It's the next day now. So where were we? Still outside, I see by reading over what I wrote.

Well, it wasn't quite as easy to get Missy Wong back as it was to bring her down. First of all, she didn't want to leave. I think she'd have spent the whole night out there if she could have. So Louise and I sort of wrestled with her, giggling semihysterically. Missy Wong laughed too, like we were playing some game.

Second of all, the security guard came by with a flashlight. Louise said, "It's okay, Bob, it's me," which reassured him because he knows Louise works there, but it was pretty clear we had to get inside. I only saw Bob that one night when Ken raged into my room, but Louise has told me about him. He looks quite intimidating, because he's a big guy with a brush cut, but Louise says he's just a goofball. He's her friend's brother.

Because Missy Wong seemed pretty unsteady on those little up-down feet, Bob got the porter to bring over a wheelchair, and he lifted her into it.

"Holy cow, she weighs practically *nothing*," he said.

That scared me, Nina. A human being shouldn't weigh "practically nothing." It's not healthy, right? She should weigh a good, solid something. I made a mental note to tell Rosie to try to get Missy Wong to eat more. In the bright hospital light, Missy Wong sat crumpled in the wheelchair. She looked desperately old now. She looked faded and tired, a completely different person than the amazed stargazer from only a few minutes before.

We all went back up to the unit, and the Night Owl pounced as soon as we got through the unit doors. She looked flustered and fluffy and red-faced as she took hold of Missy Wong's wheelchair.

"What the—where have all of you been? Do you know what time it is?"

Good old Louise. She said, "Kasey caught Missy Wong going downstairs, so she went with her and got her to come back up. I was just helping when Bob came by." It wasn't the truth, exactly, but it wasn't technically a lie either.

The Night Owl thanked me and Louise, which made me feel just a bit guilty. Louise volunteered to take me to my room, and the Night Owl looked grateful.

"Goodnight, Missy Wong." I leaned over and touched her hand. Usually she'll grab your hand in both of hers and hold on. She didn't even move, didn't even look up.

"She's exhausted," said the Night Owl. "We need a good, long sleep, don't we, little Missy?"

I watched them head down the hall. The nurse blocked Missy Wong out completely, but a corner of her shawl trailed along the floor.

"C'mon, kid," said Louise. "You better get to bed too. You look super tired." She walked me to my room, watched me climb into bed and pulled the covers up for me. "You need anything? Water? Cheetos? I can get you some Cheetos from the cart."

I laughed and shook my head.

"Yeah, maybe those would be gross right before bed," she agreed.

"Probably. Thanks, Louise." She knew I wasn't talking about the Cheetos.

She looked around the room, sighed and said she wished she could sleep in one of the spare beds rather than going home. It was strange, because just at that moment, I'd been thinking that all I wanted was to be at home rather than in the hospital. And here was Louise, wanting to be in the hospital and *not* at home.

"Maybe when I get out of here, you can come to our house, Louise," I said. "For a visit. Meet my family. It'll be noisy," I warned.

She smiled and said, "Sure, maybe."

After she left, I wrote that last letter to you, and the whole time I was thinking about families and homes. I wondered about Missy Wong, where her family was, and why they never visited, and if she thought of the hospital as a home, and us (the other patients and the nurses) as her family. And whether she thought of other people when she looked up at those stars and wondered whether they were looking at the stars too. Or were up with the stars. She must have had parents. Was she thinking of them? Maybe she had a husband, and children, and even grandchildren. Maybe even great-grandchildren. Where were they all? In her head? In the stars?

I thought of Ken, the confused old man who searched for his kitty that one scary night. Rosie told me he has a home and a family that visits him all the time. I've even seen them—a nice old lady with poufy bluish-gray hair and very white running shoes, who must be his wife, and other people who must be his sons and daughters, even though they seem older than my grandparents. It's confusing, but the sad part is that he doesn't know any of them. He doesn't remember his home.

I'm so lucky, Nina. That might surprise you after a month of letters complaining about everything in my life. But it's true. Sure, this bone disease hasn't exactly been a party, but otherwise, I'm so *lucky*. I remember my home. I love my home. I love my family. I love Squeakers. I love my bed, my messy, shared room, our noisy kitchen, the family room where you're always stepping on some toy, our concrete basement with the hockey nets and basketball hoop and giant tote of dress-up clothes. I even love our yard with the scrappy grass, the peeling fence and the swing set that jumps off the ground if you swing too high. I love my mom's singing and my dad's lame jokes, and Lizzy's facts about the life of *squids*, and Molly's bizarre and very long plays, and Kyle's being a "BIG guy!" and the baby's gummy smile and his tiny toes that are the exact size of *peas* (Lizzy and I measured).

I'm also very lucky to have a friend like you, Nina. Thanks for reading all these letters.

And for writing to me and visiting me. You're part of "home" to me too.

Your lucky, lucky friend,
Kasey
(Whose mom just dropped off a burger and fries. See what I mean? Lucky!)

Twenty-Four

Dear Nina,

It's two days since my last letter.

Are you sitting down? I never asked you how you read these letters. I always imagined you on your couch with Sheba on your lap, reading my letters while you pet her long soft fur. Anyway, if you aren't already sitting down, please sit. And grab Sheba. You might need her.

Rosie and Louise came into my room today. I knew right away that something was wrong. Louise's face is like mine—we don't give much away. But Rosie is always, always cheerful. Not today.

"What is it, what's wrong?" I asked.

Rosie sat on the side of my bed while Louise shoved her hands in her pockets and stared at the floor.

"Kasey, I have to tell you something sad," Rosie said, holding my hand. "Missy Wong passed away a little while ago. You and Louise were her friends. She was a friend of mine too. She was a dear, dear little lady, and she had a very long life. And she passed away so peacefully in her sleep."

I looked at Louise, who was studying the pictures Kyle and Molly drew for me, blinking hard.

I couldn't actually concentrate on anything Rosie said after that phrase "passed away." Such a strange phrase. Passed what? Away to where? None of it seemed real.

I'm sorry if this is a shock, Nina. It was a shock to me too. I've never known anyone who died. I didn't know what to think. I didn't know what to feel or what to say. I just felt cold.

Rosie said that my parents were coming for a visit soon so we could all go and see Missy Wong one last time.

"Could we go now? Just you and me and Louise? I'd rather go with you." My mom and dad didn't know Missy Wong like we did, and what if they brought all my brothers and sisters? No, it was better to go with Rosie and Louise. And Ivy. She knew her too.

We went down the hall to Missy Wong's room, to the bed behind the curtain. And there she was, peaceful-looking, like Rosie said. She looked smooth and still, like a little doll.

I touched her little hand that I'd held so often. So small, that hand. "Goodbye, Missy Wong," I whispered. "I hope you're going home." All of a sudden I had the wobbly feeling that my poker face was slipping. It was crumpling up. I turned, and Rosie crushed me in a big hug.

"She was getting sicker and sicker, Kasey," said Rosie. "Better this way."

"I think we should give Louise her shawl," I said too loudly. "She was so nice to her, and saved her applesauce and pudding. Missy Wong would've wanted her to have it." That shawl had comforted

Missy Wong, had been a part of her, and she didn't need it anymore.

Rosie said it was a wonderful idea and turned to a small pile of folded clothing on the chair near the bed. On top of it was Missy Wong's chart. I saw the spine, which read *Wong, Mei-Xiu*. Mei-Xiu was her real first name. She was a hyphen too! Maybe she hated the hyphen when she was a kid and decided to go by Missy like I picked Kasey instead of Katherine-Charlotte.

Rosie shook out the shawl, and it glinted and glowed in the sunlight from the window, rich turquoise and gold, brilliant red and emerald green. Then she held it out to Louise, who grabbed it and muttered, "Thanks." She looked like she was going to say something else. Her eyes met mine. But then she turned and left the room.

"Just upset," said Rosie.

"Rosie," I said, "when I'm back at home, will you look after Louise?" She said of course she would. That's what friends are for.

I thought Louise might be mad at me. Well, not really *mad* mad, but upset. But she wasn't.

Later that night, when Ivy and I snuck down the hall and took the elevator downstairs to the back entrance, there was a stick propping the door open. Louise was there, sitting with her back against the building, wrapped up in the shawl. She moved over to make a spot for me on her jean jacket.

We sat there not talking, thinking of Missy Wong and looking at the stars.

Your friend,
Kasey

Twenty-Five

Dear Nina,

Do you know the happy-sad feeling? I can't believe it, but I don't think we've ever talked about it. It sounds babyish, but it's not. It's the feeling you get in between endings and beginnings. You want to hold that ending close, close, close before even thinking about that new beginning. Like when we won the league championship two years ago. It was great but also sad in a way, because that was it for soccer for the year, and four girls moved up a division. That team was over.

The last day of school always gives me the same feeling. Obviously, I always look forward to summer holidays, but I also love school. And even when I'm really ready to be done school, I always have a moment where I think, "I'll never again be in that grade with exactly those kids and that same teacher." Do you think ever think like that?

I've got that feeling now, when I'm almost free to go home from the hospital.

I went around with Rosie yesterday and said goodbye to all my friends. Sadie smiled and nodded and asked me what's for lunch. I haven't told you much about her, but aside from her obsession with lunch, Sadie has a beautiful voice. Does that surprise you? It surprised me. One Sunday, a choir came in and assembled by the front desk. When they began singing, Sadie (who everyone thought was asleep, and who practically never says anything) sang along with them, word for word, her eyes closed the whole time. These old folks are mysteries, Nina.

Yolanda grabbed my hand and wouldn't let go. I had to pry it away and pat her on the shoulder instead. Ken smoothed his hair, tried to sit up straighter and frowned, trying to remember me.

I can't believe I was ever terrified of him. He shook my hand with both of his big, dry hands and said, "Ah, nice of you to come by, good to see you." You could tell that he felt he *should* remember me, but he didn't really. So he just relied on that deep-down politeness so many of these old people have. I can't tell you how many times they've offered me some of their lunch or dinner, for example. Even their dessert. How nice is that? They don't know how much I've loathed the food here.

We went all down the unit, and I waved to the ones who were so sick they don't get out of their beds at all. And you know what, Nina? Some of them did brighten up and smile when they saw me. I wonder if they just like children, or if they remember how fun it was to be a child, or whether I'm just different than the people they see all day. Maybe it's all mixed up together.

There's someone new in Missy Wong's bed already, Nina. She has tubes in her nose, which look uncomfortable. I don't know her at all, but she smiled and waved at me anyway.

I told Rosie it wasn't *really* goodbye. I mean, I live in this town, right? I can come and visit them anytime. And I will. And let me tell you, Nina, when I do, I'm bringing delicious food with me. I'm already thinking of homemade treats for Thanksgiving, because can you even imagine the turkey-like substance and "gravy" and wiggly, runny cranberry mush they're going to get? I shudder just imagining it.

July 19 today. Tomorrow, July 20, I begin my summer holidays! Oh, Nina, I want to do so much. I want to run outside, climb that big tree in the park, beat Dad in a race, have a water fight, eat buckets of ice cream, eat any other nonhospital food, play that stupid goofball game with you and Lizzy and Molly and Kyle, lick Popsicles, watch movies (no, not that sequel), play soccer and play tennis with Mom.

Come to think of it, while endings sometimes feel sad, beginnings are nothing but happy.

Your friend, from beginning to end,
Kasey

Twenty-Six

Dear Nina,

If my letters had titles, the title of this one would definitely be "The Last Letter." You'll notice I crossed out "The Final Letter," which sounded formal and *grim* somehow, as if I shall never again write another letter in my life.

Anyway, I'm almost free!

I'm sitting on the edge of my bed, which will only be my bed for a few more minutes. Mom and the baby are at the desk, filling out paperwork with the Bouncer, switching ownership of me from the hospital back to my parents. The TV guy came to take away that useless thing. My little bag is packed. My books are in a box. My stuffies are crammed back into a (clean) green garbage bag.

The Fussbudget came a little while ago to tear all the tape and arm hair off my arm and separate me and Ivy. Her skills have not improved.

"Little pinch," she warned, as she yanked the needle out of my hand in a burst of searing pain. Honestly, Nina, that woman should not be in charge of needles *ever*. I rubbed my hand as she picked up all the stuff that slid to the floor.

It was such a strange feeling watching her unhook Ivy's bag head, and roll up her tube arms, one of which flapped at me like a last wave. She stripped Ivy down to only her pole body and wheely feet, and as she was pushed out the door, she looked like just another piece of medical equipment. Like a wheelchair or a cart, just a piece of metal that serves a purpose. She was probably going to be shoved into storage beside that enormous, disgusting bathtub (which I *won't* miss). But she'll be pulled out again to help someone else get healthy, which is a nice thought.

It might sound crazy to you, Nina, but in my head I said goodbye to Ivy too. She helped protect me at night and stayed with me when I was lonely and scared. And she *healed* me. Hard not to be grateful for that. The nice, nonrobot doctor told me yesterday (in different, more medical words) that my bones are feeling all of them JUST FINE. So thank you, Ivy. I'll never forget you.

I rubbed my pale, sickly-looking hand, which felt strange and limp and wasn't used to being free. I experimented with opening and closing it, and it felt weak. While I'm not going to be arm wrestling for a while, it's not permanently damaged, just like the rest of me. Can you train just one arm? I wonder. One hand?

It was a great feeling to be able to slide my left arm into a sleeve! Does that sound pathetic? After a month of a bare left arm and shoulder, and clothes tucked in and bunched up and tied up, it's such a relief to wear clothes the normal way.

Mom came back from the desk and said, "You're free to go!"

⟳

Free! I could hardly believe it. I felt very strange, almost worried, about leaving my bed. I looked around my room one last time. But you know what, Nina? It was just a hospital room—four beds, four bed curtains, a window and a bathroom, all in various shades of hospital blue-green. Everything that made it *my* hospital room—the pictures, the books, the stuffies—was coming home with me. Well, everything but my germy slippers, which I threw into the garbage (as promised).

Rosie walked to the elevator with us, talking and laughing. She gave me a big hug, and suddenly we were in the elevator. Rosie is quite an amazing person, Nina. She wasn't sad I was leaving— she was happy! Happy I was better, happy I was going home where I belong. I'm going to try to feel like that when I think of little Missy Wong. Happy for her.

I'm finishing this letter in a hurry in the car while the baby is gurgling in his car seat beside me and grabbing my hair. You might see the writing has become bumpy. I want to see your face when I *hand* it to you! I hope you're home.

"Oh, what's all this?" Mom said in an innocent voice with the sound of a smile in it. I looked up.

Our street, our house coming up on the right. Balloons! A sign that says *Welcome Home, Kasey!!* My family and YOU out in the front yard, waving and cheering, and *why am I still writing*?

Your friend, who will be running out of this car the second it stops,
Kasey

Acknowledgments

As always, thanks to my editor, Sarah Harvey, who makes my books better, who champions my weird ideas and who sends me photos of her adorable grandson. Thanks also to another Sarah, my niece, for the chats about writing and for the website support. I would also like to acknowledge the real Missy Wong, who was a friend of mine when I was in the hospital for a month when I was nine years old. I hope she's dancing in the stars.

Alison Hughes writes for children of all ages. Her books have been nominated for the Silver Birch, Red Cedar, Diamond Willow, Hackmatack and the Alberta Literary Awards, as well as the Sigurd F. Olson Nature Writing Award. She shares her love of writing by giving lively presentations and workshops at schools and young-author conferences. She lives in Edmonton, Alberta, with her husband and children, where her three snoring dogs provide the soundtrack for her writing. For more information, visit www.alisonhughesbooks.com.

MORE MIDDLE-GRADE NOVELS BY
AWARD-WINNING AUTHOR
ALISON HUGHES

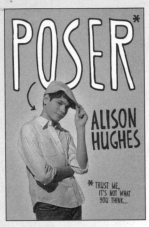

"LAUGH-OUT-LOUD
FUNNY."
—*SCHOOL LIBRARY JOURNAL*

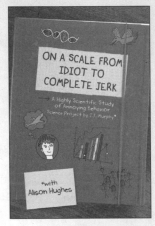

"QUIRKY."
—*QUILL & QUIRE*

"ENGAGING."
—*VOYA*

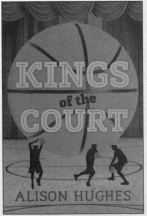

"EXUBERANTLY
MULTIRACIAL AND
MULTIETHNIC."
—*KIRKUS REVIEWS*